NOT DOWN IN ANY MAP

NOT DOWN IN ANY MAP

STORIES

P.A. Callaro

Epigraph Books
Rhinebeck, New York

Paperback ISBN 978-1-960090-52-2
eBook ISBN 978-1-960090-53-9

Library of Congress Control Number 2024902279

Some stories in this collection have appeared previously in the following publications:
"The Derev'ya Social Club" in *The Muleskinner Journal*.
"No. 2 White Street" in *Umbrella Factory Magazine*.
"Not Even Our Brothers" in *Bloom*.

Cover design by P.A. Callaro.
Book design by Colin Rolfe.

Epigraph Books
22 East Market Street, Suite 304
Rhinebeck, New York 12572
(845) 876-4861
epigraphps.com
callarofiction@gmail.com

For my family,
Stephanie
Devon
Madison
Austin
Danielle
Nora
Remy
and all who come after.

It is not down in any map; true places never are.

—Melville, *Moby Dick*

CONTENTS

NOT
DOWN
IN ANY
MAP

NO. 2 WHITE STREET

SEVENTY-SIX-YEAR-OLD Calvin T. Wright ran his hand across the ragged edges of the brick wall. His dark brown skin contrasted the dingy, painted surface. Both he and the modest, two-story white brick and clapboard house had been roughened by age, by neglect, and by the ease in which the world ignores or even abuses things and people that have earned admiration, or even reverence. His son Randolph handed him the exquisite leather portfolio with a large W embossed on its cover, which Calvin pressed to his chest. Calvin's wife was gone now, but his grandchildren would soon see this, and that brought tears to his eyes. Together, the two stood silently for a long while in something close to prayer.

Seven hours earlier, and sixteen miles to the north in his Bronx apartment, Calvin awoke, opened the window shades, walked across the now-sunlit, green linoleum floor of his bedroom, past the hallway window darkened by the proximity of the brick wall outside, and into the bathroom. He studied his ragged face in the mirror. In any cast of light, whether the harsh fluorescent above his mirror or the darkened shadow of a brick wall, Calvin T. Wright saw an obscurity, an irrelevant character in a book no one cared to read. He'd arrived unceremoniously on a rag-covered mattress in a New York tenement seventy-six years ago, and he was certain that he would depart this life at his appointed time, having contributed nothing of consequence to the world, offering no legacy, and bearing nothing of distinction to leave behind.

He ironed his white shirt and put it on. His arthritic fingers struggled with the buttons. He straightened his tie in the mirror and dusted off his suit jacket. He looked again at the letter he'd received from the attorney and tucked it into his suit pocket. As he walked out of his third-floor apartment, he stopped on the stairway to pet his neighbor's cat, Rodney. He pulled from his suit jacket a small plastic bag of cat treats that he always carried with him should he come upon Rodney lounging near a radiator or attacking raindrops as they slid down the hallway window. He stepped out into the bright sunshine, crossed 187th Street, and walked toward Fordham Road and the steps that led to the elevated train tracks.

These days, Calvin rarely rode the train. He spent most mornings at Dizzy's Coffee Shop with his pals Archie, Chico, and Maurice playing pinochle and telling tales, some taller than others. If you know what to listen for, you can learn a lot about a person when best friends tell stories about each other. Not long ago, Chico retold the story of Cal and the lavender purse. How it contained a credit card and two hundred dollars. How Cal found it, left behind on the Grand Concourse bus. How he traveled several miles to return the purse to its owner. How he lightheartedly accepted the razzing he received for carrying the accessory under his arm.

How a young hooligan attempted to separate the purse and the two hundred dollars from Cal. And, how Cal dismissed the delinquent using weapons he'd honed over decades: kind words, self-deprecating humor, and irresistible moral persuasion. He boarded the No. 4 train headed downtown to Manhattan where he would meet his son Randolph and the attorney from Schumacher & Lange.

The train rattled south, and soon Yankee Stadium, where Calvin had worked for fifty-two years as a ticket-taker, came into view. His anxiety over the letter gave way to recollections of young, wide-eyed children entering that baseball cathedral with their ball caps and gloves to watch their heroes play ball. He recalled the most precious memory of his work, the arrival of the occasional father and son from his neighborhood in the Bronx, for whom visits to the ballpark were out of reach. These neighbors were the recipients, au gratis, of two tickets for the outfield bleachers. Calvin assured them that the tickets were a perk of his job and cost him nothing. The fathers doubted this but couldn't refuse the gift. None were so inhuman as to deny Calvin the joy he received by giving it. And through their acceptance, they were given a second gift that is the birthright of every American father and son—a sun-washed afternoon together at the ballpark, courtesy of the innate kindness of Calvin T. Wright.

Calvin's anxiety returned as he exited the train in unfamiliar territory at 86th St. and Lexington Avenue. He met

Randolph at the end of the littered platform. As they hugged, Randolph unabashedly kissed his father on the cheek, a profound gesture of affection passed down by the Wright men ever since Calvin watched his father kiss his grandfather.

"Dad, can I see the letter?"

Randolph read the letter silently.

"Same as when I read it to you over the phone," Calvin said. "No details, just a bunch of legalese about some confidential matter that requires my attendance. I just hope it's not a problem with my pension."

"Don't worry about it. You just let me handle this."

They walked up the steps finding themselves in the posh Upper East Side of Manhattan. Each was dressed in a suit and tie of their own vintage. Randolph's charcoal gray pinstripe was standard wardrobe for his work as the branch manager of a local bank. Calvin's was brown with wide lapels, purchased twenty years earlier. It was his only suit and was worn proudly at all family events. He looked dapper at Randolph's wedding, pious at the baptisms of his three grandchildren, and inconsolable at his wife's funeral. Today, its worn elbows belied the grace in Calvin's steps as he and his son walked to the Fifth Avenue address noted in the letter.

The grand five-story limestone building stood across from Central Park in the affluent shade of broad elm trees that such a building required. A doorman, surprised by their approach, welcomed them, and led them across the ivory terrazzo floor to the concierge desk where, with letter in hand, Calvin and Randolph were announced on a private telephone to an attorney awaiting their arrival upstairs. Burnished bronze elevator doors opened and they were escorted to the palatial, fourth-floor, tawny oak library of the late Kerson P. Carlyle.

Far from a self-made billionaire, Kerson P. Carlyle had been the beneficiary of the shrewd dealings and privilege of his ambitious forefathers after their arrival from Great Britain in 1799 and their purchase of a small yarn-spinning factory near the Concord River outside of Boston. Over the years, more factories were added, producing fine silk and woolen fabrics that became the cargo for the family's newest investment: railroads—railroads that serviced the industrial revolution burgeoning in the country. Mr. Carlyle's great-great-grand-father would be thunderstruck. Rather than yarn and fab-ric, it was railroads that made the Carlyle family fantastically wealthy. These most fortunate circumstances, together with Mr. Carlyle's unwavering benevolence, explained his pri-vate jet, his donation of millions of dollars to feed the city's poor, his precious artwork, the Carlyle wing of a New York hospital, and his dozens of properties scattered across the globe. What they could not explain was the presence, in Mr. Carlyle's grand library, of a 76-year-old Black gentleman from the Bronx and his son.

The starched attorney from Schumacher & Lange had the face of a gravedigger. He was seated behind a cus-tom-made Louis XVI desk of persimmon wood the color of ebony and was flanked by a junior assistant. On the desk was a framed photograph of Mr. Carlyle shaking hands with President Lyndon Johnson. Calvin glanced at the painting above the fireplace. The ticket-taker from the Bronx didn't know it was Cezanne's *Mont Sainte-Victoire*, but over his seven decades, he'd come to know other things. As he gazed at the blue-gray brushstrokes that formed a mountain, he knew that this painting was not one to be displayed in a Bronx apartment house.

The attorney stood and invited Calvin and Randolph to make themselves comfortable in two crimson colored Chippendale wing chairs upholstered in fine Carlyle & Co. herringbone silk. A butler poured coffee, pleasantries were exchanged, and the attorney, in comforting and deliberate tones, produced Mr. Carlyle's last will and testament, which included a letter and articles from the deceased that were to be disclosed only in the presence of Mr. Calvin T. Wright.

It could have been any of the morning's events or surroundings—the Fifth Avenue mansion, the private elevator, the photograph of presidential privilege, the Cezanne—that raised their suspicions. So unlikely was their presence in this scene of opulence that Randolph couldn't contain a sudden eruption of laughter, imagining the *real* Calvin T. Wright— the longstanding, close family friend with grand expectations of sudden wealth at the demise of "Uncle" Kerson—who was surely the intended participant of this solemn ceremony.

Recognizing Randolph's outburst as a benign skepticism regarding their presence at this gathering, the attorney attempted a gentle smile and assured Randolph that there was no mistake, that his father was, in fact, the correct Calvin T. Wright, and that once he shared Mr. Carlyle's letter and associated articles, the mystery behind this improbable meeting would vanish. The attorney finished his legal pronouncements and shared Mr. Carlyle's materials and expository letter. For the next fifteen minutes, the Wrights learned of the incredible discoveries made during Mr. Carlyle's final months, which did indeed explain it all.

Among the vast assets collected over the years by Mr. Carlyle and his many business entities were several New York City properties, including a modest, two-story white brick and clapboard house located at No. 2 White Street at the corner of West Broadway in downtown Manhattan. Beyond the date of its construction in 1809, much of its 213-year history was lost to the fog of time. For the past sixty years, the building had been rented to shopkeepers in one trade or another. Several months ago, during the repair of a water leak in the basement, a metal box the size of small briefcase was found behind heavy stones that had become loose in a basement wall adjoining the furnace. It was the discovery of this box that set in motion this day's events.

The attorney placed the rusted box on the desk and opened it. He removed a rubber sheath containing a notebook with the date 1843 stamped on its frayed cover. Perhaps owing to the protection of the rubber sheath and the warm, dry climate behind the furnace, the notebook's binding had held together quite well. Most of its pages, however, were torn or effaced beyond legibility, leaving readers to speculate about their contents; yet, several pages had survived in miraculously clear form, showing distinct handwritten columns of names, conductors, arrival and departure dates, modes of transportation, and travel routes with destinations to the north in New Hampshire, Vermont, and Canada. Of special note, was the first page of the notebook, only half of which remained intact. All that could be discerned was the address, *No. 2 White Street, New York,* the words *Station Agent,* and the station agent's signature in elegant cursive that read only

Reverend Theodore Sedgwick, which was followed immediately by an illegible smudge of ink and the frayed edge of the torn page.

The attorney continued, following the instructions of the deceased, by reading verbatim a quote from Mr. Carlyle's letter. "There are places and times in this world when certain acts of courage and humanity must be performed in deepest secrecy, and when the danger that necessitated their concealment is past, these acts demand our awareness, our gratitude, and our reverence. Sometimes however, such goodness remains obscured for far too long simply because the world cannot agree on what is good."

Everyone in the room, none more than Calvin and Randolph, understood the history of the Underground Railroad: the station agents and conductors who, unlike those similarly titled in Mr. Carlyle's employ, engaged only the machinery of the soul. Father and son were astonished at this incredible historical document but still confused over Calvin's presence at this now almost spiritual proceeding. Before either could raise his voice however, the attorney continued, explaining that upon hearing of the notebook's discovery, Mr. Carlyle spent his last months unearthing with vigor the truth of the courageous affairs performed at grave risk inside the modest white brick and clapboard house at No. 2 White Street at the corner of West Broadway, 175 years ago.

From the box, the attorney removed two additional items, items not ravaged by time. He placed on the desk first a deed of ownership bearing Calvin's name for the small, white brick and clapboard house at No. 2 White Street. Next was a cashier's check drawn from the estate of Mr. Carlyle, to be paid to Calvin, in the amount of $8 million, to be dispersed as he saw fit for the repair and proper maintenance of the historic house.

It had become too much to bear. Randolph stood in disbelief. His father had never heard of Kerson Carlyle until the letter arrived the previous week. Once again, before Randolph could speak, the attorney placed the final item on the desk, and his tone became one of veneration. It was an exquisite leather portfolio with a large W embossed on its cover. Inside was a genealogical register drawn on parchment papers with the magisterial elegance of a calligrapher. This historical record had been created with the considerable influence and connections of Mr. Carlyle. It was to be a legacy for future generations of the Wright family. The ancestral line began with the present-day grandchildren of Calvin Theodore Wright, of the Bronx, New York, and traced back through six generations of Calvin's forebears, to the 1797 birth of Calvin's great-great-grandfather, Theodore Sedgwick Wright, in Providence, Rhode Island, who in 1828 was ordained as the Reverend Theodore Sedgwick Wright.

The reverend's full name was no longer obscured by the smudges of time, or torn paper, or human neglect, and Calvin T. Wright was no longer an obscurity. Beneath the reverend's name, the document affirmed that until his death in 1847, Reverend Theodore Sedgwick Wright resided in New York City, in the modest, two-story, white brick and clapboard house at No. 2 White Street at the corner of West Broadway.

ESMERELDA AND
THE QUEEN

THE man with the long dark beard reeked. He shuffled along the shady side of the street smoking the nub of a used cigarette, never far from the rusted wagon overflowing with his life. He was part of the grit that I could see and feel and smell in the streets around my home in the Bronx. The diesel fumes, the sleight of hand between dealer and user, the broken windows, the chronic vacant lots, the gray soot from the auto body shop, all of it settled in like a cruel neighbor invited by a determined neglect. I passed the bearded man as I walked to the El train that thundered above Jerome Avenue. I tried to think only of the train and where it would take me, but he wouldn't leave my thoughts, the man with the beard who deserved better than the hopelessness stuffed into so many of his torn plastic bags.

As I climbed the stairs to the train platform at 170th Street, the grit disappeared but not the hopelessness. Today, it was my turn to ride the 4 train. Far down the tracks, headlights appeared, not steadfast and certain, but quivering like a mirage in the impossibly hot early September morning. Mirages, and their bolder cousins, lies, need to keep their distance so you can't touch or feel them or see them up close for what they really are.

The train arrived, and, once inside, I found the cool air soothing, but, like the shimmying headlights, it was a lie too, as if the train were an express that could shuttle me to the fair air and clean waters of Canada or Maine. But right there, close enough to touch, the hostile red and green graffiti on the walls of the train was truth—one that wasn't fair or clean.

I took a corner seat for the fifty minute ride south, pulled out my phone, and listened to Beyoncé's *Renaissance*. Queen Bey sang about escape, a hard thing to find in this part of the Bronx, so I'd decided to look for it in Manhattan. Papa had looked for it too, for him and Mama when they were young, but both lies and truth got in the way.

Early that morning, as she was leaving for work, Mama held my shoulders with outstretched arms, and with a doleful stare and shake of her head, she fastened the top button of my blouse. She smiled with satisfaction, I, with acceptance. She gave me a hug, straightened the barrettes in my hair and kissed me on the forehead.

"That's better. *Mucha suerte*, Esme, I hope everything goes well."

"*Gracias*, Mama. I'll see you tonight."

She slammed our apartment door, thick with too many layers of paint to close smoothly, and walked to the B train that would take her to Mr. and Mrs. Hoyt's brownstone in the leafy Upper West Side of Manhattan where, to Mama, the sky seemed bluer than in our neighborhood. This was their first day back from their annual summer retreat at Cape Cod.

Mama had recounted her daily routine at the Hoyts' many times over the years. Mr. Hoyt would already be at his office downtown when Mama arrived. Mrs. Hoyt's three young girls would shout, "*Buenos dias*, Mrs. Iguarán," and wait for Mama to smile and return the greeting. Mama and Mrs. Hoyt would chat about matters that needed attention and other news: maybe the girls' dance lessons after school or a nail polish spill in the upstairs bathroom or the health of a cactus plant Mama and the girls had planted in June in the rooftop garden, or my National Honor Society award at St. Angela's High School. They'd write the to-do list, and Mrs. Hoyt would kiss the girls goodbye and go to work upstairs in her office with a view of Central Park. Mama would make breakfast: organic brown eggs and fresh fruit for the girls and for Mrs. Hoyt, coffee and a kale smoothie in the Vitamix whose color matched the Viking range in the vast kitchen. After breakfast, Mama would walk the girls to the Beresford School on 75th Street, where the sidewalk ginkgo trees, untroubled by police sirens, shaded the children as they entered. Then she'd return to the house where laundry and the rest of her day's work waited. Mama felt blessed by her job with the Hoyts, but she always told me that her real job was the one at home holding our family together, even though it was just the two of us now.

When Papa was young, he thought college was the way out of his family's tenement and he had politely shared his thoughts with his father.

"I'm good at drawing, Papi. I could study architecture or engineering."

The response from his Papi came in machine gun Spanish with little concern for his son's impractical dreams. "And where will we get the money for college, Miguel? The coffee shop that *we* will own. That will be our work."

Though he loathed his Papi's traditional thinking and lack of imagination, all my young Papa could say was, "Yes, Papi. I'm sorry."

Papa was sixteen when he quit school and with it, his hope for college and his search for liberation. But escape can be cruel and unpredictable; sometimes you search for it and sometimes it searches for you. He rode the 4 train to Manhattan where the office buildings had enough floors to wax and bathrooms to clean to keep Papa a prisoner for life. Thirty years riding this train from our third-floor walk-up on 170th Street to the Chrysler Building wearing an ID card clipped to his company-issued beige uniform that paired well with his deep cinnamon Cuban skin and accent. There never was an Iguarán family coffee shop. It was just another distant, seductive mirage whose lie was fixed in the hopelessness of this place. They told us he slipped and hit his head on the slop sink in the janitor's closet on the forty-sixth floor. Papa was forty-six years old.

In my corner seat on the train, I fastened a clip to my new ID card and looked at the picture on it. A smiling Esmerelda Iguarán stared back, another in the Iguarán family with cinnamon skin, this one with a small gold cross around her

neck—a gift from Papa that was never, ever removed—
fine brown hair pulled back into a bun and studious round
glasses framing determined brown eyes. I clipped the card to
my worn Key Food Market tote bag.

Living with dirty elevated train tracks is accepted in the
Bronx, but the high-rise condos of Manhattan were spared
the greasy gloom outside their floor to ceiling windows. As it
left the Bronx and crossed the Harlem River into Manhattan,
the elevated 4 train, as if ashamed of its own commonness,
descended below ground, hidden from view as it rumbled
under Lexington Avenue.

They got on at the 86th Street stop, talking as they boarded.
Both were tall like Miss Teen America contestants in ripped
skinny jeans, NYU T-shirts, and spotless running shoes.
Miss 86, with long, straight blond hair, porcelain skin, and
a button nose, and Miss Lex, with short red hair and silver,
mirrored aviator glasses. They tossed their Fjällräven backpacks on the floor, sat in the corner seats across from me,
and continued talking just loud enough to be heard by the
passengers around them.

"Saturday night, after we went back to the house, did you
see Jeremy and Lucy sneak back to the beach?" said Miss 86,
as she used both slender hands to toss her long hair behind
her shoulders.

"Yeah, Lucy said she's obsessed with him. She said
they've been doing it for weeks, at her beach house, at home
in the city when her mom and dad are working, basically
everywhere. Her mom's clueless," said Miss Lex.

I looked down at my phone, trying not to care as they chattered on about family vacations, new jewelry, and their recent pedicures. I had cool ripped jeans at home too.

Mama screamed the day I brought them home from the store. "They're ripped! New jeans with holes?"

"Mama, they're what everyone wears now."

"No, no. You can't wear these Esme. Please, don't."

"Mama, why are you so upset? They're just jeans."

Watching my mother as she put her palms to her cheeks with a heartbreak in her eyes that I couldn't comprehend, I felt my lower lip quiver and couldn't stop the flow of my own tears. In the little we ever had, Mama and Papa could always find something valuable to hold up to friends and strangers, things well-known to hard-working janitors and maids but not always to their children. They weren't things you could buy. They were things that would define us, the Iguarán family, as decent, proud, worthy, respectable. In that moment I realized that my vanity had betrayed those things, the most valuable things Mama and Papa ever possessed. I kept those ripped jeans—they're still in my closet—but I've never worn them.

As Beyoncé sang, I could sense Miss Lex, behind her aviators, staring. I was looking at my phone, but I saw it, the slight nudge of her elbow against Miss 86's arm, never taking her mirrored glare off the stale and faded supermarket tote bag resting on my lap. Their muffled laughs through lip gloss smiles and Upper East Side derision were as obvious as their shocking blue nail polish. I was three feet away, close enough to feel it. It was the same at the night spots in Manhattan.

Girls from the Bronx or Queens were part of the BTC, the Bridge and Tunnel Crowd. The exuberant colors of our clothes, the audacious spirit of our jewelry, even the freedom we expressed in the way we shared a joint in the alley behind our favorite dance club were shocking to girls with penthouse views. Our mere existence in Manhattan was shocking.

At 14th Street, we all switched to the local 6 train. We stood together as the doors closed. Miss Lex was searching for something in her backpack as the subway car lurched out of the station, and she dropped a plastic card. I faked a wobble and placed my worn leather shoe directly on her card. I bent to pick it up and saw the solemn image of Miss Lex, without the shield of her mirrored aviators, on her New York University ID card.

"I've got it. Sorry, I think I may have stepped on it by accident."

"Yeah, uh huh."

I smiled as I handed it to her, imagining that I heard a thank you. One stop later, at Astor Place, I followed the two out of the subway into the sunlight of lower Manhattan. They walked west down Waverly Place, ten steps ahead of me. At Greene Street, Miss 86 glared over her shoulder at me as they both turned and entered one of the NYU buildings that dominated the area. I returned a scowl of my own, used my middle finger to push up my glasses on my nose, and continued past the NYU building, walking west on Waverly until I arrived at Washington Square Park.

It was 8:40 a.m., and I still had twenty minutes to kill. I walked into the oasis of grass and trees surrounded by a desert of concrete and steel. Tall linden and locust trees guarded the park's winding paths. I sat on a shady bench at the south side and looked north, past the fountain whose spouting water provided a cooling mist to passersby, to the white marble Washington Arch that towered over students making their way to class on this first day of school. My high school AP History teacher, Mr. Campbell, once explained that the Romans built grand stone arches to celebrate great victories. Napoleon too, after his victory at Austerlitz, built the Arc de Triomphe, which could have been the model for the arch now in my view. The Washington Arch celebrated our first president, but today, I decided it would also celebrate a victory.

It was time to go. As I stood up, I noticed a familiar and intense aroma. In front of a handsome new building at the edge of the park was a beat-up 1960s era VW minibus. It was painted red and green with neat lettering that read CUBAN COFFEE KING. I grabbed my tote bag weighted with books and walked toward the handsome building whose name was now close enough to see—NYU College of Arts and Sciences. In my ears, Queen Bey was singing about discovering a new foundation and the salvation that came with it. I stopped at the VW for a coffee, and as I reached into my bag for my wallet, I clipped my ID card to the inside of the tote so it wouldn't fall out.

THE DEREV'YA SOCIAL CLUB

И толь'ко здесь' я обречен на страдать,
И толь'ко здесь'—к спокойствию.
—Лермонтов, *Мой дом*

And only here I'm doomed to suffering,
And only here—to calmness.
—Lermontov, *My Home*

THREE men watched Alexei Petrovich Ivanov enter. He removed his cap, scratched his cloud-white whiskers, took a seat at the bar, and politely asked the barman for tea and *sushki* biscuits. He turned and nodded at the three men with a satisfied smile as one of the three, an old man with a thick gray beard, rose from his seat and moved toward the bar.

The Derev'ya Social Club in Brighton Beach, Brooklyn, was opened in 1951 by two Russian brothers nostalgic for the cafes of their homeland. Its main room was thirty feet square, with small black and white hexagonal floor tiles. Along the rear wall resided a long mahogany bar, home to two enormous brass samovars both cast in the image of double-headed eagles, an homage to the great Tsars of Russian history. At one end of the bar stood a carved bookshelf filled with chess sets, the latest editions of the newspapers Novom Svete and Vecherniy and dog-eared volumes of Lermontov, Chekhov, and Tolstoy, many printed in Russian. At the other end was an upright piano, on which, during cold and dreary days reminiscent of the Russian winter, a skilled patron might delight the room with a Rachmaninoff Prelude. On the walls, Stravinsky, Plisetskaya, and Gorbachev looked on as their compatriots nibbled their biscuits. In the center of the room were tables, each with a glass vase holding flowers picked from the outdoor garden in the rear of the cafe where glorious planetrees provided guests with dappled shade and the club with its name: Trees. Uneven stones paved the garden where its main feature, an eight-foot tall marble fountain, was crowned with a bust of Tchaikovsky. Metal tables, benches, and heavy wooden pedestals inset with stone chess boards looked up to the maestro as pews would an altar. For the older Russian emigres, Derev'ya was a soothing refuge, a sentimental tribute to the beloved motherland, an agreeable place that blissfully erased time and distance. For those of the new generation in Brighton Beach curious about their Russian heritage, it was a living chronicle to ensure that the time of great Russian culture and enlightenment would not be forgotten.

As the hot tea melted the memorable biscuit in Alexei's mouth, the bearded man approached him. "Hello, may I inquire if you are you new to the Derev'ya?"

"Yes, I am," Alexei said. "I am new to Brooklyn as well, but as of today I am a member of this fine club."

"Well then, allow me to introduce myself, I am Leonid Asimov, but you can call me Leo."

"It's a pleasure to meet you Leo, I am Alexei Petrovich Ivanov, but please, call me Alexei."

Leo invited Alexei to his table where the other two men were now standing to greet the stranger.

"Gentlemen, I'd like you to meet a new member of the club, Alexei Petrovich Ivanov. May I introduce Ivan Belsky, and this is Ivan Grumov. Long ago we gave up the confusion and they became Belsky and Grumov."

Eyeing the frayed and yellowed collar of his shirt, the two men shook hands with Alexei.

"It's my pleasure to meet you all. I'm very happy to now live near a café like this. In the Bronx, I had no such place nearby. To Derev'ya, I can walk in minutes. And I must say, the ginger biscuits are heavenly," Alexei said.

Leo shook his considerable stomach. "That is the work of Mrs. Solokin. She runs a serious kitchen and is not one to be trifled with. When it's known that she is making her apple blintzes, it's so busy here, you can't get in the door."

"Yes, I think you will like Brighton Beach much better than the Bronx," Belsky said.

Leo offered Alexei a chair. "Please, join us."

"I don't want to interrupt your conversation," Alexei said.

"It's no interruption, we are three old men talking about nothing. We are happy to meet a new neighbor of similar age," Leo said.

"Thank you, I share the sentiment," Alexei said.

"So, you say you live nearby? Belsky asked.

"Yes, I live with my sister Vera near the glove factory on Neptune Avenue."

"Ah, Leo, he lives not far from you," Belsky said.

For the next hour, over tea and Mrs. Solokin's sweet *pastila* cakes, the men, in a pastiche of Russian and English, shared their stories from the old world and the new.

In 1931, Alexei Petrovich Ivanov was born in the small village of Dubishki, Russia. Now seventy-seven years old, he praised the *sushki* biscuits at Derev'ya, which were almost as sweet as those he shared with his father each Sunday morning of his childhood. Young Alexei idolized his father, a man of culture who always carried some book of poetry in his suit pocket. He earned meager wages writing for the local newspaper and spent his leisure time with the educated class, discussing music, language, books, art, and writing poetry. In the evenings, he tutored his children in English and played symphonies on his phonograph. He read to Alexei and his younger sister Vera at bedtime. Often, it was Pushkin. Young Alexei was ill-equipped to comprehend the verses of *A Magic Moment I Remember*, but he was spellbound by the emotion in his father's voice as he read the closing lines: "Then came a moment of renaissance, I looked up—you again are there, a fleeting vision, the quintessence of all that's beautiful and rare." They lived a civilized and artistic, if frugal, life. Alexei would never forget his father's words that *material* things are transient, but that which is in our hearts and minds will last forever.

Twenty-two years later, with Vera already settled in Chicago and nothing left in Russia for his heart to embrace, Alexei and his new wife Anya moved to America. With the assistance of a professor in St. Petersburg who knew his father, a job as a schoolteacher was arranged in the Russian community near Pelham Parkway in the Bronx.

Anya gave birth to a son, Pyotr. Complications made additional children impossible, which made Pyotr all the more precious. After college, Pyotr found great success as an American entrepreneur. Alexei showered his fellow teachers with reveries not of his son's success, but of the walks in the park with grandchildren that would surely come one day. But how could he know? There was no foretelling of a horrific railroad accident. Russia's subjugation had taken his mother and father and now America's liberties had taken his wife and his son, and with them, his hope for a grandchild. He became an inconsolable recluse, darning his own socks, writing the occasional letter to his sister Vera, leaving his small flat only for work, or for groceries. Sitting by his open eighth floor window, he contemplated his own end. In this, he may have succeeded were it not for the resolute love of his sister Vera, who could read both the feigned contentment and the unwritten sadness in her brother's letters and who invited him to share her new home in Brighton Beach, Brooklyn.

With the dinner hour approaching, Leo, Belsky, and Grumov tossed notes on the table to pay their checks. Alexei, under the curious eyes of the others, opened a small, ragged cloth purse, removed several coins, and counted them precisely before placing them on the table.

As they walked to the door, Leo said to Alexei, "Perhaps next time we play a game of Durak, you can join us. Do you play? We can always use a fourth player."

"One moment please," Alexei said, as he walked back to the table to retrieve his cap. Grumov and Belsky frowned at Leo, unsure that an invitation to join their card game was appropriate for a man they had just met.

Leo whispered, "Weren't you listening to him? He's wonderful. He will be an excellent addition to our group."

Alexei returned with his cap and answered, "I would be delighted to play with you, but I must warn you, I am a remarkably poor player. You may wish you never invited me."

The sound of old men coughing through their laughter was heard by all as the four friends left Derev'ya and breathed the salty ocean air, each pleased with this new beginning.

Over the following years, Alexei spent his mornings walking along Brighton Beach Avenue under the roar of the El trains conversing with shopkeepers and making pennies appear from behind the ears of the neighborhood children. On warm days he would cross the boardwalk, remove his shoes, and feel the sand between his calloused toes, picking up errant trash as he walked. On Wednesdays he stopped at Saint Nicholas church where Mrs. Meladova, the former librarian, attended morning services. Alexei would bring her a few *sushkis* and push her wheelchair to the boardwalk so she could see the ocean that so lifted her spirits. After lunch at home with Vera, he would nap and then walk to the Derev'ya for tea and a few verses from Turgenev under the shade of the planetrees. Soon, his friends would arrive, and stories of younger days would be told, the day's gossip would be broached, a chess match offered, and perhaps some vodka would be drunk. During these years, the four

men shared a deep contentment with life and their friendship. But the world turns, and for some, the blessings of
America—charity, freedom, conscience—compete with
darker visions of selfishness, pride, and bigotry that reside
in their hearts.

One September afternoon at Derev'ya, the four sat for tea
in the shade by the fountain and Leo asked, "Alexei, when
you were a boy in Dubishki, did your family travel often to
Moscow?"

"Dubishki," Alexei said, "is halfway between Moscow
and Leningrad and a great distance from both. There was no
money for family trips. But my father did travel to Leningrad
to be in the company of the writers and professors at the
university."

"Each to his own, Alexei," Grumov said sternly, "but I
believe the proper name is St. Petersburg."

"Pardon me, you know it's an old habit from my youth,"
Alexei said.

"Yes, a habit you make no attempt to correct," Grumov
said, unable to hide his irritation.

"My apologies, I will try to remember," Alexei said.

"So, your father was a professor at the university?" Belsky
asked.

"No, my father was a journalist by trade, but truly, he was
a poet," Alexei said. "He enjoyed the company of the writers
and musicians and philosophers at the university. He would
return home inspired and would write poems and then he
would recite them to Vera and me."

Leo smiled, "How wonderful, to be a child and hear

poetry in your father's voice. You haven't told us much about your father, Alexei. Did he ever come to America?"

"No, he did not. He died in Russia."

"I'm sorry," Leo said.

"I believe all of us have lost our fathers. How old was he when he passed?" Belsky asked.

"He was a young man," Alexei said.

"Was he killed in the war?" Grumov asked.

Alexei looked to the floor and gazed at his shoes in need of polish. Only Leo sensed his discomfort, "I think perhaps we can change the subject."

"No, I don't mind the question." Alexei said. "We have been friends for years."

"Are you sure?" Leo asked.

"Yes. After the war, a party official in our village with a strong dislike for my father accused him of stealing and had him sent away. I was fourteen years old, but I knew this was a lie; everyone in the village knew my father could never do such a thing. But the hatred had always been there; the Nazis only added to it. And when they were driven out, the hate was uglier, as if that was possible. My father was sent away and shot not because he was a thief, but because he was a poet . . . and because he was a Jew."

The air between the men was still, and, as Alexei's lip quivered, Leo said, "I am very sorry, Alexei. You must have a great deal of pain and anger inside."

Alexei breathed deeply and said, "I was angry for many years, but my anger consumed me and left no place for the beauty of the world to touch me, the beauty that my father shared with me and Vera through his poetry. My anger was a victory for the hate, and I refused to allow it to conquer me."

"Your philosophy is admirable, Alexei. I would have difficulty myself," Leo said.

"Yes," Belsky said. "It was a terrible time; it's best to forget it and move on."

"Yes, best to move on and look ahead," Grumov said.

There was a halo of sadness around Alexei when he said, "It's true, I have had my share of tragedy and I have missed my family terribly. But, in music and art, in my father's poetry, and my years of friendship with all of you, I have found great comfort and hope. At my age, I have only one regret, and that is not having a grandchild to love, to teach, to share poetry, and to carry on when I am gone."

"I know your feeling," Grumov said. "My grandsons are the sunshine of my life even when they disobey."

"Yes, they are delightful children. I so enjoy seeing them here at the café," Alexei said.

"My daughter lives not ten blocks from here, but I don't see my grandchildren as much as I would like to. Perhaps if the new playground is ever completed, all our grandchildren will spend more time here," Belsky said.

At that moment, Alexei stood, politely asked for his check, and said, "Gentlemen, I think it is time for me to leave you. Vera is making a pot roast tonight, and it is best eaten hot. Please enjoy the evening."

Alexei departed and Leo could not contain his anger.

"You both should be ashamed of yourselves. To hear him speak of his lost family and then to carry on about the joys of your own grandchildren was vulgar. How could you be so cruel?"

"So, we must never speak of our grandchildren again in his company? He is not the only one who lives with sadness.

Our families also knew the atrocities of Stalin and the Nazis. But the son of the great Russian poet from the university at *Leningrad* expects pity with his stories of heartbreak," Grumov said.

"Leo, in your old age, you are taken in by his manipulations like a fool," Belsky said.

"Can any of us imagine his heartache? He has always been a man of deep emotion and kindness, yet you both treat him like someone who is trying to steal from you," Leo said.

"That would not surprise me either," Belsky said.

"What does that mean?" asked Leo.

Belsky answered, "You see the way he reaches into that filthy old purse to pick out coins to buy one biscuit for himself. I can't remember the last time he bought tea for us. I don't care if his father was a penniless poet. Leo, do you remember when Grumov invited us to dinner at Matryoshka after he won at the racetrack and Alexei was happy to join us? But, when we returned to the restaurant a month later, he could not come. Do you know why? Because he knew he would have to pay his own check."

"It's his nature," Grumov said. "The man is a miser. Will we ever see the day when he buys a new suit coat, or at least patches to cover the holes in the one he wears every day? And all these years, he lives with his sister. Why does he live there? We've all tasted her blinis, so we know it's not for the food."

Belsky and Grumov roared with laughter.

"No, it is so he can pay half rent," Belsky said. "And I'm also tiring of his air of superiority. Did you hear him last week giving me advice at the chess board? Not as a joke, but a return to his role as schoolteacher. He sits and thinks and thinks and thinks again. Such a strategist. He beats me because of my boredom as I wait for his next move."

The two howled again with laughter.

"I'm sorry you both feel this way," Leo said.

Winter came and Grumov and Belsky saw less of Leo and Alexei. When the four were together, the chill in their words matched the cold sea air.

On a cold but windless Wednesday morning, Leo joined Alexei for a morning walk along the beach.

"Leo, have you noticed a change in Belsky and Grumov recently?" Alexei asked.

"What do you mean?"

"Things seem different when we are together, like Chekhov's student who feels a cold wind blowing inappropriately."

"I don't know, Alexei. Perhaps it's just the annoyances of old age. Maybe they aren't feeling well."

"Yes, perhaps. I will light a candle for them at St. Nicholas."

"Yes, my friend, I know you will."

In March, Grumov and Belsky were conversing at the bar when Leo walked in.

"Good afternoon, Leo," Belsky said. "You're late today."

"I have bad news from Vera. Alexei was taken to the hospital this afternoon. It is serious; he is in a coma."

"Do they know the cause? Belsky asked.

"The doctors are not sure. Vera said she could not wake him from his nap. She called the ambulance, and they took him away."

"Had he complained of any pain? Grumov asked.

"No, no complaints. The doctors are doing tests and hope to know more later today."

"Should we go to see him?" Belsky asked.

"Yes, we probably should go, if he can have visitors," Grumov said.

"Only family members can see him now. Perhaps tomorrow he will improve, God willing, then we can visit him."

Mrs. Solokin placed May flowers in the vases on the tables near the bar. In the garden, no sunlight could penetrate the clouds, and the leaves of the planetrees were dark. Grumov, Belsky, and Leo sat near the maestro drinking tea and eating honey cakes. Belsky dealt the cards, and they played Durak in silence with one empty chair at the table.

The door to the garden opened and out ran Rachel Belsky.

"Grandpa, will you come with me to the new playground when it opens later?"

Belsky spread his arms, "Of course I will, *malyshka*. Come give Grandpa a hug. Is your mama with you?"

"No, Mama is working, Mrs. Sergeyevna is with me. She says they will make the ribbon at three o'clock and then we can go on the playground, and you can push me on the swing."

"Yes, yes, *cut* the ribbon, and then you can swing. Anything you want, *malyshka*."

"Thank you, Grandpa. I'll see you later, at three o'clock. Don't forget."

"I won't forget."

Belsky turned to Grumov. "Will your grandchildren be at the playground for the opening?"

"Are you joking? They have been waiting three years for this day. They will be there," Grumov said.

"I'm sure my little ones are at the playground already, waiting," Leo said with a wistful smile.

When the time came, the three men walked to the new playground. Three years of bureaucratic red tape, something Russians understand well, was finally at an end. A sea of young children with their parents, grandparents, and nannies were gathered for the ribbon cutting. The playground was the size of a city block, filled with swings, slides, jungle gyms, and even spray fountains to splash water on hot summer days. Dozens of planetrees shaded the perimeter. At the center, a three-foot square wood replica of a house stood on a short pedestal with a sign that read BIBLIOTECHNY. It had large doors that swung open to reveal dozens of books for the children to read and borrow, plus volumes from immortal Russian poets and writers for the pleasure of the parents and grandparents.

A city official stepped to a podium for the ceremony. Before he cut the ribbon, he unveiled a bronze plaque with the playground's dedication which he read:

PUSHKIN PARK
Dedicated to the children and grandchildren
of Brighton Beach—
Our hope and our future.

The City of New York Offers Its
Sincere Thanks to the Park's Benefactor
ALEXEI PETROVICH IVANOV
1931 - 2013

IN LOVING MEMORY OF
AYNA NIKOLEVNA IVANOVA
&
PYOTR ALEXEYEVICH IVANOV

Belsky and Grumov stood silently, their faces expressionless. Leo wiped tears from his eyes. Mrs. Meladova, who had helped fill the small wooden library wept openly. Later, in Derev'ya's garden, the three men were having tea when Vera appeared.

"Vera, I had no idea Alexei was involved. What a wonderful gift to the children and tribute to his . . ." Leo was unable to finish.

"He had quietly arranged with the city to pay for the park several years ago," Vera said.

"If I may ask, where did he get such a sum to build a park?" Belsky asked.

"His son left him everything. Alexei was never at ease with gaining riches from the death of his son. He would have burned it all to get Anya and Pyotr back. So, he quietly gave it away, first to the library and then to build the park. He asked me to keep his secret. But when he died, I asked for the dedication plaque to include their names."

"I understand that he would give money to the library, but why to a playground when he had no grandchildren to use it?" Grumov said.

Vera explained softly, "His most precious hope was to have a grandchild, but he knew it was not to be. That other children would find joy in the park and be touched by the books and the poetry as he was, that was his wish."

"Vera, I will never forget him. Your brother was a man of decency and virtue," Leo said.

Leo looked at Grumov and Belsky and asked, "Wouldn't you agree?"

The two men nodded in agreement, and raindrops began to fall, but none reached the gathering thanks to the broad leaves of the planetrees.

THE ARRIVAL OF
MISS EMILY DANIELS

Away from small and youthful lark,
What thoughts think we of tender age,
Of sadness seen, utter and dark,
That plague the man on Captain's stage.

—Marianna Arrington

SATURDAY, MAY 15

MELODY Allen was enchanted by pretty things: art, poetry, young animals, wildflowers, the sound of an acoustic guitar. She was a daydreamer and often conjured places she might live one day, lush green valleys surrounded by snowy mountains or silent deserts in varying shades of brown. These places had the power to possess the 15-year-old. Her face was soft and triangular with high, blushed cheeks upon which sat round, frameless eyeglasses reminiscent of another time. Sitting in her bedroom below a poster of the Grand Canyon, Melody placed a green peace sticker, off-center and slightly tilted, on top of the large sunflower she had drawn on the flap of her canvas backpack. Her Bohemian ankle skirt was the color of the sky, and she wore buttercups, taken from flowerpots on her windowsill, in her flowing black hair that fell past her shoulders.

She opened her backpack and pulled out a well-worn book of poems by Edna St. Vincent Millay, a pristine math textbook, and a checklist of materials she needed for her project—posterboard, heavy markers in six colors, glue stick, index cards—and called to her mother in the bathroom. "Mom, are you ready to go? The store closes in thirty minutes."

Melody's mother was looking sideways into the mirror applying blush. "Melody, I don't have time to take you right now."

"Mom, you promised you'd take me so I could finish it by Sunday."

Silver hoop earrings were next. "Honey, if you had started your project when you got the assignment, you wouldn't need to rush now."

"I started last week. The pictures and drawings were easy, but I didn't understand how to do the research part, and it took longer than I thought it would. But it's done now, and I'm ready to put it together on the boards. Please, Mom, can we go now?"

"Why in the world would you waste time with artwork and drawings in a history project? Really Melody, sometimes I just don't understand your thought process. And, if you didn't understand the research part, why didn't you ask someone for help?"

"Mom, I asked you to help me, last week, twice, but you had a tennis game one time and were going to the mall with Mrs. Monroe the other."

"Melody, you know darn well I'm not the person to ask

for help on things like this. Your father was the one who handled school projects. You should have called him. You could have taken your bike to his apartment. I'm sure he could have helped you if he wasn't too busy with his . . . whatever."

"He's on a business trip, remember? And he doesn't come back until Sunday night and the project is due on Monday."

Mrs. Allen looked at her watch with exasperation, "Melody, it's not my fault that your father . . . had to . . . that he travels, and it's not my fault that you procrastinate."

"I know, I'm sorry, Mom. Can we please just go?"

"Just once, I wish you'd have a little respect for *my* time. It's Saturday night, I'm meeting Joan and Rebecca for dinner, and now I'm going to be late because of your disorganization."

"I'm sorry, Mom. I don't want you to be late. Can we go tomorrow morning?"

"You know I have tennis on Sunday mornings, so no, that won't work. Melody, sometimes you can be such a disappointment. Get your things and let's go now. I'll just have to be late for dinner."

Melody left the bathroom, and Mrs. Allen closed and locked the door. She sat at the vanity for a moment, motionless, bent over, staring at the floor. She lifted her head and glared into the mirror. Her lower lip began to quiver.

Your father!

She wiped her eyes and reapplied her mascara.

WEDNESDAY, MAY 19

Every inch of Bernard Malchek's face colluded to form a human distress signal.

He placed three large posterboards against the wall of his history classroom as Sylvia Tanger, the assistant principal, walked past his doorway.

He shouted toward the door, "Sylvia, Sylvia, take a look at this."

"Hi, Bernie. What is it?"

"Look at this kid's project from Monday's Civil War presentation."

She studied it. "Wow, pretty colorful."

"Not only colorful, but the bottom half is completely fabricated."

"Huh?"

"The biographies and dates are fine, but see those letters written to Lincoln, below his picture? They're fake. The girl just made them up, pure invention."

"Are you sure?"

"You know, when I read them, they just didn't sound right, and there are no footnotes, so I googled them every which way. I couldn't find any record of these letters, or any person named Marianna Arrington."

"Who's the student?"

"Melody Allen, you know, the hippie with the long black hair and peace signs."

"Melody! What did she say about the letters during the presentation?"

"First, I asked her why she made it look like an art project. I mean, look at it, pink circles dotting the *i*'s, squiggles, colors, curlicues. The girl stared at the photo of Lincoln, in a daze. Finally, she snapped out of it and said something about Lincoln always looking depressed, so she thought some color and fun designs would help cheer up the presentation. Then I asked her about the letters. She said they're copies, so I thought she'd copied actual letters that were written to Lincoln. Then, she said lots of people must have written letters to Lincoln to cheer him up. Can you believe it? She thought it'd be okay to make up a bunch of stuff in a history presentation."

"What are you going to do?"

"I'm giving her an F, and I'm going to ask Jenkins to suspend her."

"Really? That sounds a little rough. She's not a bad kid. Maybe you should go easy on her."

"She's a flower child with her head in the clouds. She thinks the world is all cupcakes and dancing. She thinks she can just make stuff up in a history presentation. I'm calling her mother for a meeting. I'm gonna give this kid a dose of reality."

"Well, I'd go slow. Maybe there's some reason behind it. Let me know how it goes." As she was leaving, she turned and asked, "Any word from NYU on your application?"

"Uh, yeah, no good. Strike six. Let's see, my grades could have been better, my doctoral proposal was too vague, GRE scores could have been higher. Same bullcrap, different school."

"I'm sorry, Bernie. What are you gonna do?"

"Nothing. That's the last one; I'm done. Screw 'em all."

THURSDAY, MAY 20

Janitors were cleaning Mr. Malchek's room, so he held the meeting with Mrs. Allen and Melody in the English classroom belonging to the newest teacher in the school. He sat at the teacher's desk while Melody and her mother sat in students' chairs facing him. Melody read to herself the exquisite script on the blackboard: *Tomorrow's reading assignment 19th Century Poets. Emily Dickinson: If I Can Stop One Heart from Breaking* and *Walt Whitman: Oh Captain! My Captain!*

"Mrs. Allen, I've asked you here to discuss your daughter's Civil War presentation. It contained two letters supposedly written to President Lincoln." He handed her a copy of one of the letters and read it aloud.

June 1, 1864

Dear President Lincoln,

My name is Marianna Arrington, I live in New York City. I wanted to write you a letter because I thought it would be good for you to hear some words of encouragement from an ordinary citizen. I've seen recent photographs of you and I am worried because you look very depressed. At first, I thought it was the war that was saddening you, which is completely understandable. I'm sure it's on your mind all the time with so many young boys dying and all those poor slaves who've lost hope. Recently, I read an article saying that your own son Willie died two years ago and your second child, Eddie, died in 1851, at age 3. What terrible losses for you and Mrs. Lincoln to bear. I am certain now that losing two

sons is as much a cause for your sadness
as this terrible war. When my dad left us
two years ago, it was awful, and I prayed he
would return. I've been sad ever since he
left. I realize that is nothing compared with
the death of two children. I wish I lived in
Washington DC so I could visit the White
House and hug you and tell you that you
are the most courageous and inspirational
person I know. I hope this deathly war
ends soon and we are victorious. Perhaps
then you can smile. I know God is by your
side and so am I.

With sincerest respect and hope,
Marianna Arrington

"I researched these letters and Marianna Arrington, and
I couldn't find any reference to any of it. Miss Allen, I'd like
to know where these letters came from."

Melody took a deep breath, "Well, actually, I . . . I wrote
them myself."

Like a hungry alligator stalking a wounded bird on a
pond, Mr. Malchek snapped, "Miss Allen, are you admitting
that you invented these letters?"

"Yes, Mr. Malchek, but I just thought—"

"Miss Allen, this was a history assignment."

"Yes, I know—"

"You committed a serious infraction of the rules of schol-
arly research." he added, enjoying the gravity in the sound of
his rebuke.

"But I researched a lot of information about the war and how slavery was the main reason for it and—"

"Yes, and if you had confined your work to the facts, we wouldn't be sitting here right now."

"I'm sorry. I didn't think it would be a problem. Like I said on Monday, he looked so sad, people must have written to him, with the whole country depending on him, the slaves, the soldiers dying, his own children dying." Her voice cracked. "Someone *must* have written letters to comfort him."

"Yes, yes, I'm sure. That's very decent of you, Miss Allen, but I'm lowering your grade from B to F, and I'm recommending to Principal Jenkins that you be suspended from school on the grounds of poor ethical judgement."

Mrs. Allen took a deep breath, raising her eyebrows as she looked at her watch and said, "I don't understand what all the fuss is over a couple of made-up letters. Everything else in the project was good enough for a B grade. She made a mistake; can't you just take the letters out? She understands it was wrong, don't you Melody?"

"Mrs. Allen, part of my job is to prepare my students for the rigors of college. Your daughter's deliberate falsification is unacceptable." Mr. Malchek glowed in righteous indignation as he ended the meeting and walked to the principal's office.

Mrs. Allen fumed, allowing Melody no respite from the attack as they left the building. "Melody, what in the world were you thinking? I'm completely humiliated over such a stupid thing."

Crossing the parking lot, Melody imagined it as the loneliest desert in the world.

TUESDAY, JUNE 1

The incident had been put to rest, and the weather was warming up. The park behind the Allens' house was built for quiet reflection and the enjoyment of nature. There were no swings or jungle gyms, just green lawns, many trees, a wide footpath around its edges, and a section at the far end with an old cemetery. Mrs. Allen enjoyed jogging on the footpaths, and Melody spent Saturday afternoons daydreaming under the linden trees, eating fruit from her canvas backpack.

By three o'clock, Mrs. Allen had wrapped Melody's gift and placed the supermarket birthday cake in the refrigerator. The gift promised by Melody's father hadn't arrived, something about a shipping delay by the store, but she didn't need to hear his excuses. It wasn't the first time he'd forgotten, and it wouldn't be the last. After dinner, he'd call from wherever he was, and sing Happy Birthday and ask Melody how school was and then he'd have to hang up because he was so busy with work. After dinner, Melody would go to her room and write in her diary using the fountain pen that she had taken from her father's briefcase before he moved out.

With the cake and gift ready, Mrs. Allen put on her running shoes and walked to the park for a jog. As she approached the footpath, she saw in the distance at the edge of the old cemetery the silhouette of a girl with the same long dark hair as Melody's. She saw the girl stand up, look in her direction, and place something in the grass before walking off. By the time Mrs. Allen arrived at the cemetery, the girl was gone. The graves were surrounded by ancient trees, and the grave markers were small and flat, level with the grass. A few feet from where she stood was a white envelope with a small bouquet of wildflowers lying on a copper grave marker blessed with verdigris. She picked up the envelope and read the name on the marker beneath it—

Marianna Arrington
June 1, 1849
April 3, 1947

She opened the envelope and removed a card with a note written in youthful script.

June 1, 2021

Dearest Marianna,

They didn't like the letters in my presentation, but it doesn't matter. I liked them and I know you would have too. I hope you don't mind that I signed your name on them. In 1864, you were the same age as I am today. Maybe you really did write a letter to President Lincoln. I'd like to think that you were the kind of person who would. I hope it's okay if I stop by now and then to say hello.

Happy birthday.
Melody

The *i* in Marianna was dotted with a pink circle. Mrs. Allen put the card back in the envelope and turned to leave, the envelope in her hand. When she reached the path, she heard footsteps on the twigs behind her. She turned but saw no one. She thought for a moment and walked back to the grave. She placed the envelope and flowers back on Marianna's grave and walked home.

THURSDAY, JUNE 3

She was twenty-five years old and the newest teacher at the high school. She had met Melody only a few times in the cafeteria and was impressed by her soft-spoken kindness. After the incident with Mr. Malchek, she visited Mrs. Jenkins and asked what had happened. She listened to the story and learned that Melody's grade wasn't reduced and she wasn't suspended. Mrs. Jenkins explained that Melody's misstep didn't come from a reckless disregard of the rules, but from her empathetic heart. The presentation was still in the principal's office, and the young English teacher looked at it closely. The girl had managed to take the most horrific war in American history and add a whimsical lightness that was terribly inappropriate yet somehow forgivable.

"Did you read the letters?" Mrs. Jenkins asked.

"Yes, I did."

"Marianna is quite a creation, wouldn't you say?"

"Yes, she is." She returned to her office and called Mrs. Allen to arrange time for a meeting.

MONDAY, JUNE 7

Miss Emily Daniels arrived at the Allen house at four o'clock. Mrs. Allen answered the door wearing a blue tennis dress and holding a tennis racket.

"Hello, Mrs. Allen. I'm Miss Daniels from the high school, Emily Daniels; we spoke last week on the phone. Is this still a good time to talk?"

With an unconvincing smile, Mrs. Allen said, "Yes, please come in. It's fine; my game is at five. This won't take long, will it?"

"Ah, no, I'll be quick."

"Great."

Mrs. Allen showed Miss Daniels to the living room, and they sat on the sofa.

"Is Melody home?"

"No, she's out."

"I'm glad everything worked out with her presentation. I'm sure she realizes now that a history presentation is not the place to be creative with facts."

"Oh yes, lesson learned."

"I saw Melody's presentation in Principal Jenkins's office last week."

"Look, if you don't mind, I'd really like to forget the whole episode."

"I'm sorry, Mrs. Allen, I'll get to the point. In addition to English, I teach a summer writing workshop at the high school. I was hoping that Melody might sign up."

"Miss Daniels, I read Melody's letter. I didn't think much of it, but it certainly sounded fine for a 15-year-old. I really don't think she needs a writing tutor."

"No, I'm sorry, that's not what I meant. Mrs. Allen, has Melody written anything else, stories, other letters, a diary maybe?"

"No, I don't think so, nothing like that. I mean, you know, maybe a birthday card whenever, but nothing else I'm aware of."

"Mrs. Allen, did you read the second letter that Melody wrote for her presentation, under the name of Marianna Arrington?"

"No, I didn't and honestly, I don't want to rehash it now."

"It'll only take a minute. I brought two copies; I really think you should read it."

She handed her a copy and they both read it in silence.

April 8, 1865

Dear President Lincoln,

I hope you received the letter I sent to you last year, June 1st, 1864. Since then, I've spoken to many of my friends at school and at church, and they thought I should write you another letter of support. I told them I would, but I decided to write you a poem instead. Even though I wrote it, it has the spirit of all the kids at school and church in it. So, you can think of it as a poem from all the children of America who love and admire you. We want you to take our hand.

Take Our Hand

Away from small and youthful lark,
What thoughts think we of tender age,
Of sadness seen, utter and dark,
That plague the man on Captain's stage.

Youth, legion we are, United anew,
One hand all to soothe your pain,
With God's strength and faith imbued
In you, His victory will remain.

Marianna Arrington

Melody's words, the words of a 15-year-old girl surrounded by dissension and anger yet wishing only for har-
mony, had brought Miss Daniels to tears. What must Melody
have felt to write a thing of such beauty, with such depth
and humanity? Mrs. Allen looked at the letter, and at Miss
Daniels, and again at the letter, and with a restless expression
she said, "Okay, I get it, she made this up too. Can you please
tell me what you want Miss Daniels?"

"I want to help her."

"Help her with what?"

"Do you know who Marianna Arrington is? Is she a
friend of Melody's?

Mrs. Allen hesitated, "Uh, no. No, I don't know who she
is."

"For a girl so young, to create such a character and write
with such compassion is a wondrous thing."

"So wondrous that it almost got her suspended."

"That was unfortunate, Mrs. Allen, but your daughter has a unique gift. With some coaching and practice, she could be extraordinary. She should be encouraged to write, to express herself through writing and poetry. I'd like to help her."

Mrs. Allen looked at the teacher and took a long, deep breath.

Miss Daniels smiled softly and said, "Melody has something special inside her. But I'm sure you know that."

Mrs. Allen gazed out the window as if searching for something. She folded the letter and looked at her watch.

THE COLD ROOM

THE boy's father believed a man was defined by two things: his work ethic and his family. This man was a workingman of tradition and honor. He taught his son to show respect not only to him but to all the virtuous men of their neighborhood, many of whom were veterans of the war who now provided for their families in jobs building and maintaining the city. It was important to him that he be seen by them as a diligent father whose children dressed neatly, earned good grades, and above all showed respect to the adults in their community. The boy was taught to listen before speaking in the presence of his father and the principled men of their community—the shopkeepers, the policemen, the priests. These were the teachers of life.

For 13-year-old boys in New York City in 1974, a cool spring Saturday morning during the school year meant a game of stickball. The boys toted baseball gloves, broomsticks, and a pink Spauldeen rubber balls to the street. Bases were drawn with chalk; if chalk wasn't handy, parked cars and manhole covers were acceptable substitutes. Pitches were thrown, home runs were hit. Soot fouled their faces, but the impossible city sunshine cleansed their attitudes.

For this boy, family obligations had no respect for stickball games. He had other duties to attend to on Saturdays, so his baseball glove remained in the dusty space under his bed as he carried only his disappointment down the steps of his apartment building, up two blocks to the subway, and across four stops on the D train.

The family bakery was a small shop on a busy corner of a neighborhood built by Italian and Irish immigrants a century earlier. His father never directly asked the boy to work at the bakery on Saturdays. The boy divined this filial duty himself, not through some magical discernment of youth but through the suggestive comments of his mother and by careful attention paid at the supper table where, as his mother cut his meat, he would observe his father's thick fingers caressing the corners of his mouth, full of clenched teeth, whenever the conversation turned to the fraught fourteen-hour workdays of an approaching weekend. Work ethic and strength of family, not stickball, were the foundations of character, and the boy could not disappoint. This was the cost of the respect owed to his father. He would work at the bakery on Saturdays for a tiny allowance until his younger brother was ready to take his place.

He was sixteen when his brother replaced him at the bakery, and he began a search for a summer job that paid a real wage. Now, the subway took him downtown where a massive new grocery market displaying a "Now Hiring" sign was about to open in an old disused warehouse. His father's lessons of respect and politeness had good effect, and he was given a job paying two dollars per hour in the store's dairy section selling milk, cheese, and eggs.

Mr. Zimmer was thirty-four years old with roughened hands that suggested he had once worked at a job involving concrete. After his army service and years of work at jobs he despised, he saved enough money to open a small hardware store, but larger competitors and a greedy landlord forced him to close his shop. He set aside his bitter disappointment and accepted the job as manager of the grocery market. His unhappiness could often be seen in his face, but he worked hard and maintained his sense of obligation to his employer. The boy recognized Mr. Zimmer's qualities as those his father would admire.

On the boy's first day at work, Mr. Zimmer introduced him to two other boys he'd be working with for the summer. Becker was an unimpressive boy of seventeen with a chubby face, crew-cut black hair and round eyeglasses whose only talent was his slavishness toward the older boy. Ellis was eighteen but he looked older. He drove his own car with hand-painted pinstripes. He was tall with eyes that spoke a confidence that could either assure or frighten those around him. When Mr. Zimmer had gone back to his office, Ellis and Becker brandished a box cutter and backed the boy against the wall explaining that Ellis was the boss when Mr. Zimmer wasn't around. Mr. Zimmer's melancholy may have blinded him to the unsavory character of these two delinquents, but the boy's eyes were now wide open.

The boy quickly regarded Mr. Zimmer to be an excellent

boss and teacher. Likewise, Mr. Zimmer found the boy a will-ing, pleasant, and competent worker. Each day, Mr. Zimmer gave the group a work list for the day, and each day Ellis gave the more objectionable tasks to the boy.

The cold room was where milk, cheese, and other perishables were stored. It was kept at 38 degrees and became the pre-ferred summer hideaway for Ellis and Becker to avoid both the heat and their work. Their indolence and threats of vio-lence angered the boy, and he was tempted to report them to Mr. Zimmer, but the box cutter deterred him.

On one brutally hot afternoon, the boy ate lunch at the shaded picnic table in the store's front parking lot. It was the sort of heat that created a magical shimmer on the distant asphalt, a mirage of undulating waves whose spell controlled everything—signposts, cars, people—in its torrid realm. After he'd finished lunch, he walked back inside and wondered why the cold of winter had no such power to distort reality.

The boy walked to the cold room for a few crates of milk to fill the display case. The chill was a welcome relief. He heard muffled voices coming from the rear of the room and a noticed a pungent odor in the air. Smelling the foreign odor reminded him of another he had encountered several years earlier among a group of teenagers drinking from paper bags on the street corner. Their whiskey had a pleasant musky smell, and he wanted to ask the teens about it, but guilt over-came him. He thought of his father's rage if his involvement with these teens ever became known to him. He escaped the scene before any neighbors could see him.

The odor in the cold room hung in the air with an exotic

mellowness that was different but no less pleasant than the whiskey. As he moved to the back of the room, he saw the Ellis and Becker reclining on a pallet smoking a cigarette. As he drew closer, he could see it was not an ordinary cigarette. He'd never seen a joint before but had heard about the handmade shape and funky smell. Here in the cold air, the shimmering curves of smoke from the illegal weed were no asphalt mirage. Becker and Ellis laughed high and loose between drags, and they debated whether to offer the boy a hit or keep it all for themselves.

Recalling that street corner years ago, the boy turned quickly as if reminded of an important assignment and hurried out of the room. He was stunned. This was beyond laziness; it was a shameless disregard for the law. Ellis and Becker were breaking the law, right here in the store, during working hours, only steps from Mr. Zimmer's office! The boy heard the voice of his father, the words repeating over and over: Disgraceful. Disrespectful. Criminal. He set aside his fear and strode to Mr. Zimmer's office.

Mr. Zimmer was on the phone in a cheerful mood. He saw the boy approaching and asked him to wait outside. As he stood in the hallway, doubts emerged. They could be fired, possibly arrested. Was he ready to face the wrath of Ellis and Becker after their punishment was dealt? He thought of his father, and he knew this was the right thing to do. His conviction became an eagerness to leave behind his station in life as a boy who needed his father's lectures to remind him how personal actions define one's character. He entered the office and began to perspire. His mind was committed but his face was creased and somber. Seeing this, Mr. Zimmer's expression and mood became one of concern as well.

"Is something wrong?"

"Sir, I was just in the cold room, and I need to tell you something."

"What? Is it the compressor?"

"No, it's ..."

"Tell me what's wrong."

"Ellis and Becker are smoking marijuana in the cold room."

Here he was, a boy of sixteen, acting on the fervent lessons he had been taught all his life, engaging in a thing that was equal parts rectitude and betrayal. Was he to be celebrated for his maturity or despised as a rat? He dismissed any feeling of guilt for exposing his co-workers and instead praised himself for having done what his father would undoubtedly call the right thing.

Mr. Zimmer responded with irritation and offense. "Seriously? Damn Ellis. I told him to let me know when he brings weed to work. Are they still there? I'll be back later."

Dreams can feel lifelike. As Mr. Zimmer shuffled out of the office to get high, life became dreamlike. Sweating in the warm and stagnant office air, the boy's mouth hung open in silence. Was this real or another heat-induced mirage? It was as if while studying a cherished textbook with the codes for a virtuous life, he had turned a page and suddenly all that came before was a staggering lie. If the rules of life were nothing more than ephemeral notions to be discarded when some more attractive rule appeared, then what *could* be trusted?

He left the store that evening and his eyes stung with despair and disbelief. The subway car was crowded, but its cool air chilled his skin and cleared his mind. A man wearing dusty canvas overalls and a flat cap pushed past a woman to take the last open seat. Above the man's head the boy saw advertisements that he had never noticed before. They were tattered and marked with graffiti; one advertised life insurance, another, mortgage loans. He read them several times as the train rumbled homeward, not understanding.

When he arrived home, his mother was setting supper on the table. She took her seat next to his younger brother while his father, sitting at the head of the table, began his familiar exhortations on the events of his day—his introduction to a fine new neighborhood policeman, his delight at the creation of a Shopkeepers Association, the ordination of Father Calidus at their church. The boy removed his baseball cap and noticed a black smudge on the white NY stitched on the front. The boy put the cap away. He washed his hands and sat down opposite his father. He filled his plate and ate with cold indifference as if the room were silent.

DEGREE OF DIFFICULTY

THE basement had its own entrance, a pullout sofa, bathroom, and mini kitchen. I didn't pay rent; instead, I cleaned the house, grocery shopped, and did the lawn work.

Most mornings, we had breakfast in the upstairs kitchen: toast, juice, conversation.

"It's forty-two thousand, not forty-eight thousand," I said.

I was right, but it was a small victory. He had me in his headlock of logic that predicted that I was doomed to decades of paying off my student loans because no one made real money with a degree in English. My double major in sociology only amplified my questionable decision-making. I'd end up working as a teacher or a librarian, or worse, a bartender, living with a roommate and making barely enough to get by in New York City. Okay, he had a point; a job as a social worker paid thirty-six thousand dollars, and I'd need more school and more loans to earn the advanced degree needed for a better paying teaching job.

"The big money," he said, "is in engineering, computers,

and business, not teaching English or doing social work. You should have studied business."

"I didn't want to study business. And who says you need a business degree to get a good-paying job in business? You think everyone who works in advertising or sales has a business degree?"

"Maybe so, but even if you get a job in business, you'll be competing with finance guys and slick marketing types. They're all salesmen, numbers guys—you're not a numbers guy. You don't think like those people. They're sharks."

"Dad, that's old-school thinking. I have other skills. Businesses kill for people who can write well, who have good people skills, good communications skills. And did you know that reading fiction teaches skills that businesses want—"

"Yeah, like what."

"Like understanding people, their motivations, their viewpoints. That's a valuable skill in negotiations or when working in teams. I can learn the business part on the job."

"They're sharks, they'll eat you alive."

It took a few months to land it. I wasn't tending bar, but it wasn't exactly a job in "business" either. Most mornings, when I got to the office by eight thirty, my work would be piled in my cubicle—updates to the database, customer letters to log, reports to be filed. My salary as an insurance company research assistant was about the same as a social worker's, a fact I tried to keep from my father. I think he knew, but he never mentioned it. Four months of filing and sorting was all I could take. I began searching for a new job.

I waited for the "I told you so" speech, but all he said was, "Don't worry, there are plenty of better jobs out there. We'll find one."

Three months later, I was selling advertising space for a magazine publisher. My father hugged me, appreciative of my determination, but he still gave me the speech about sharks eating me. I wasn't deterred. In fact, I managed to last a whole year in those shark infested advertising waters, enjoying the few occasions when I was named a Top Performer in monthly sales meetings. But when budgets were cut, I was let go. I reminded my boss of my performance; we argued, and I slammed his door as I left. So much for understanding the viewpoint of others. At home that night, I geared myself up for my father's "hungry sharks" lecture.

"How many months did you make their Top Performer list?" he asked.

"Three times in the last six months."

"For a new employee with no sales experience, that's pretty solid."

A few weeks later, I saw a post online for ad sales jobs at the Paradise TV streaming network. Armed with a Top Performer attitude, I was hired by the vice president of sales, with a bigger salary than at the magazine. At my year-end review, I ranked first among all the rookie salespeople, and I was given a raise. I practically floated through the door as I arrived home that night.

"Dad, you're looking at Paradise's top rookie salesperson, and I got a big raise. Whatd'ya think of that! I'm making almost double what I was making at the magazine."

His eyebrows moved up on his forehead, a familiar sign of surprise, shock even, but he recovered and said, "That's fantastic. Good for you."

"Dad, I think I'm going to look for my own place."

"Why? Why not stay here, rent free, at least for a while? You be able to put a big dent in your school loan."

"I know, Dad. It would be great to save the money and pay down my loans, but my job is awesome. I can afford rent *and* my loan payments. You've been great letting me live here for free. Thank you for that. But I need to have my own place. You understand, don't you?"

He smiled with closed eyes as if recalling a distant memory. "What, it's not cool living in your father's basement? Okay, if that's what you want, but you better come by for dinner once in a while."

"Absolutely. I will."

I left the house filled not only with pride for finally being on my own, but with gladness for not calling him out for mistaking his son for shark food.

By the end of my second year, the vice president who had hired me was moving into her new, third floor office with a plaque on the door that read, Miriam Maxwell, Executive Vice President. Thanks to my phenomenal rookie year and my ability to discuss classic novels and writers, Miriam had not only promoted me to sales director, but had granted me the added title of protégé, a designation that provided a welcome sense of security considering she possessed what could politely be described as an idiosyncratic personality.

Anyone called to her office for a meeting could witness it. Even the furniture shared Miriam's attitude. The massive low slung sectional sofa wore supple Italian leather in a shade called Dominion Onyx. Against the wall were imposing eight foot tall wooden bookshelves that stood like sentries disarming visitors with their striking polished veneers. She would close her office door by remote control, and subordinates summoned to the EVP's office were instructed to sit in black silk chairs in front of her glass desk, the chairs positioned just low enough to allow Miriam the ability to look down on their occupants. Fresh flowers made a failed attempt to moderate her only interpersonal skill—intimidation.

It was only when successful or wealthy CEOs or entrepreneurs visited the office that Miriam took on a more reticent tone, that hinted at some inner psychological ache. Then, roles reversed. Miriam sat behind the transparent desk, but now, it was the student looking down at a teacher in the black silk chair; an impostor hosting real leadership. Her weak, obsequious smile was magnified by its reflection in the glass. The office, too, was a mere reflection, filled with wood veneers and leather hides masquerading as soaring oaks and champion bulls.

In social settings, Miriam's personality expressed itself in her carefree pretensions, as if they enhanced likeability. She never missed an opportunity over lunch to correct a junior executive's misguided opinion of some novel or work of art. Her delight was palpable at the company Christmas party when she announced, in an overwrought French accent, that the composer of the Christmas Oratorio was not Camille *Saint-Saens*, but Camille *Say-Sohnz*.

Two years of continued success in the shark tank, evidenced by another raise and a new red BMW, not only freed me from my father's headlock of logic, but it bred an indifference to Miriam's pomposity. It was good to be king, or at least the protégé of the queen, and I was enjoying the perks, like the early morning chats in her office where conversation revolved mostly around events in her social calendar and listening to her analysis of the latest Pulitzer-winning novels.

One memorable exception was the day we watched an interview on the television in her office. A women, who looked remarkably like Miriam, wearing a sharp black blazer and white blouse, was answering questions about her company's financial results. Miriam silenced me with a raised finger and became rapt with her twin on the screen. A protégé, if attentive, becomes a proficient interpreter of his mentor's expressions and body language, and as Miriam watched the interview, I sensed in her equal amounts of sisterhood and envy with her twin. Both were well-educated and successful businesswomen. Miriam was enchanted with her twin's acuity with language, her confident style, her sharp wit and intellect. But I had no doubt that the most beguiling aspect of her twin radiated from the three capitalized letters after her name at the bottom of the screen. Miriam unconsciously read it aloud, "Robyn Vance, CEO of Sportx Corporation."

As the interview went to commercial break, and the screen dimmed, so did Miriam. Some fantasy of power had faded along with the blackened screen. All I could see in the sleek office was Miriam behind a glass desk that couldn't hide her noxious envy of those three capitalized letters.

Retirement was sure to be comfortable for Emily Green, thanks to her brilliant business instinct, generous company stock options as CEO, and shrewd investments. Years ago, when Emily launched Paradise TV with wheelbarrows full of hedge fund money, she insisted on being involved with even the smallest decisions. Eventually, the company's growth forced Emily to hire more staff.

It was then that she stumbled upon Miriam, a woman with no experience in advertising, video streaming, or managing large organizations. She'd studied art history in college and later started an interior design company which, due to the combination of disinterest in niggling details like training and communication and a less-than-stellar facility with the financial balance sheet, she managed to bankrupt. While numbers may not have been her primary strength, she was articulate, a gifted conceptual thinker, and highly motivated. That was enough for Emily since she would never be far from any financial decision. Miriam was hired as vice president of sales, and after years of company growth, she ascended to her large third floor office as EVP of sales and marketing, a position that, in her view at least, made her heir apparent to the 68-year-old CEO.

The leather sofa had barely been used when Miriam hired George Butler to fill her old job as vice president of sales.

My new boss was tall and sleek with tortoiseshell glasses and Hollywood good looks with dark hair and a sprinkle of gray at the temples. Impeccably dressed at all times, George was a skilled talker with a disarming sense of humor. He came to the job with an MBA in accounting and decades of experience in sales. He was someone my father would call a shark. I had another word for him.

In all the time I worked for George, I never heard him dispense a single innovative idea of his own on how to grow our business. No papers or folders were ever seen on his desk, and meetings in his office mostly revolved around humorous stories from the good old days. He did, however, apply maximum effort to creating the illusion of work by regularly walking around the building with an anguished expression on his face, rubbing the whiskers off his chin as if he were engaged with some looming business catastrophe, making sure everyone in the building saw him obsessing over the incredible pressures of his job.

But George Butler was as shrewd as he was lazy. Even laziness, when coupled with New York street smarts, could take a guy a long way working for a boss uninterested in the details of managing people. And so, with Miriam duped by his illusion of competence, George got down to the important work of becoming Miriam's shameless lickspittle. He ran for Miriam's early morning coffee, fetched her sweater during meetings in the chilly boardroom, and arranged tickets to whatever event Miriam and her husband desired, all part of his elaborate insurance policy to protect the financial gravy train he'd stumbled into at Paradise TV.

At first, her offer seemed a lovely gesture, then it felt like a bad idea. This sort of thing always managed to leak out, becoming a topic of conversation around the water cooler.

"That's very nice of you, Miriam," I said, "but I've already got plans. My dad is cooking and the whole family is coming, so I have to pass, but thank you so much for the invitation."

"Sure, I understand. I knew it'd be a stretch on Thanksgiving. I wasn't sure if you had plans, but of course I understand. I hope you have a nice Thanksgiving with your family."

The following January, I received another raise and a new invitation from Miriam, this one for myself and a guest to join Miriam and her husband at the symphony. Then in April, another, for a night of cards with the Butlers at her house, and in August, a tennis game at her club with some of her old school friends. After the previous Thanksgiving invitation, I had recalled a line in an old movie, "Don't shit where you eat." I decided then that, although I had no choice but to put up with Miriam's inferiority complex and ambition and pomposity at work, I didn't have to endure it on my time. I decided it was best to keep my work and personal lives separate and let my work performance determine my success. I found polite and innocuous reasons to decline the symphony, the cards, the tennis, and prayed against another Thanksgiving dinner invitation from Miriam. Instead, I spent the year focused on earning another raise, fantasizing about a bigger apartment, and imagining the bitingly humorous idea of surprising my dad with two round-trip tickets to the shark infested waters of the Bahamas.

The office was a beehive of activity in early November with overtime hours, skipped lunches, even sightings of paper on George's desk. By the Monday before Thanksgiving, everyone had mentally closed shop. I was enjoying lunch and the *New Yorker* in the cafeteria when George's assistant, Alma, waved me down. I was certain something important was up; George was lazy, not malicious.

"He wants to see you."

"Right now?"

"Yes, he said now."

I dumped what was left of my lunch and walked to George's office.

"Close the door, and have a seat," he said.

"Let me guess," I said. "It's about the pitch to Sportx, right? Miriam's been after them for a while."

"We're terminating you," he said.

I looked at George's face and recalled my childhood dentist, an old-school, 75-year-old who didn't use Novocaine. As he drew a picture showing me how he was going to drill my cavity, I began to faint, but he caught me before I fell out of the chair. George didn't use Novocaine either, but he wasn't going to catch me.

"What?"

"I'm sorry, but yes, we're letting you go."

"Why, what did I do?"

"You didn't do anything wrong; this is not for cause. Every year we look at the overall performance of every employee, and we assess their future potential with the company: are they progressing in the right direction, are they stagnant, or are they regressing. Your sales performance was good, but management feels that since your promotion, you haven't been developing in an upward direction. So, we're letting you go."

Management feels. How bloodless that sounded. Suddenly, all my years of success was being erased by a mysterious disease I'd contracted, some lack of progression.

"I can't believe this. I'm having a great year. I've never had a negative comment on my annual reviews. How can you just fire me like this?"

"A person's sales record is just one element we look at. It doesn't excuse anyone from meeting the company's overall performance goals."

"George, if you thought there was a problem with my development, why didn't you say something months ago, instead of firing me out of the blue?"

He pursed his lips and took a deep breath, moving his head slowly from side to side. "Look, I like you. Really, I do, so I'll be straight with you. It's never just about sales, it's also about attitude. Powerful people . . . expect things. We all have to learn to do whatever's necessary, whenever, and wherever, to stay in the game, 24/7, even if it's uncomfortable."

I was too angry to process what he had just said. "And what does Miriam think of this?"

"This wasn't my decision, Miriam signed off on it before leaving town. I'm sorry. You have until five to clean out your cubicle. You'll get the standard severance package of one month's salary for every year of employment."

Back at my desk, I boxed up my personal items including a photograph of Miriam and me holding the trophy for winning the egg race at our company picnic.

"*It's not just sales . . . powerful people expect things . . . do whatever's necessary . . . even if it's uncomfortable.*"

I walked out of the building looking forward to Thanksgiving. Our family would gather at my father's house and stay for the weekend. We'd watch movies, obsess over a puzzle, eat too much, and feel grateful. Thanksgiving didn't have any of the duplicity of Christmas, whose true meaning, a joyful celebration of humanity, was at odds with what it had become, a business opportunity perverting and commercializing the word *gift*. Thanksgiving was about people, about family and friends, about gratitude.

I turned the ignition on my red BMW. I was rewarded with the throaty grumble of the engine. The box holding the remnants of the last three years was in the seat beside me: a coffee mug, an old picture of Mom and Dad, some knick-knacks, a framed photo of a ridiculous egg-shaped trophy, and crammed, wrinkled, into one side of the box, several Salesperson of the Month awards. I smiled as I put the car in gear and drove to my father's house.

A SEDUCTION
OF OLEANDERS

SHER

THE sunny voice on the loudspeaker reminded the crowd to "stand clear of the closing doors," but provided no advice for the uncertain rider who became clamped in the closing jaws. A different voice, no less cordial, announced the next stop like an elementary school teacher explaining what a noun is. Seconds later, someone was rudely jolted backwards as the car left the station. We were riding a congested, thundering flume which, if you avoided eye contact, could also be a place of meditative solitude. Those unacquainted with the New York City subway might find these incongruities unpleasant. But even after four years of college at NYU had transformed me from a country rube to an adroit city navigator, this rumbling underground beast, this loud, grimy, teeming lifeline of liberation with stops at the most exhilarating cultural, historical, and artistic locations in the city, remained a gratifying paradox. Through its dark and breathless tunnels, this girl from Vermont could still see the bright colors of her dreams.

The Amtrak train that took me home for school breaks had its own strange alchemy. It transformed the wide green hills of Vermont, which had enchanted me as a young girl, into a stifling pastoral monotony where beauty became drear and my exuberant New York life faded from my memory. The stout trunks of the fir trees now seemed like the bars of a cell door, and the revered Vermont country roads, flirting their dogbane and evening primrose, so beguiling to visitors from Europe or El Paso, were just maddening pavement traversing trite covered bridges.

For spring break, I abandoned Amtrak and flew home to Burlington using money I had earned waiting tables. This indulgence, rather than eliciting pride for my strong work ethic, annoyed my mother. When I had left home for my freshman year, she agreed to pay only for train fare home, consigning me to seven hours of lower back pain. This was her cruel strategy to illuminate the unpleasant consequences of my impractical and unwise decision to attend college in New York City rather than in Vermont, which would have kept me closer to home and, more importantly to her, my clinging and repressive mother. It's true that in high school, I'd taken pleasure in declaring my independence from her oppressive maternal grip by not applying to any colleges in Vermont. And yes, once at NYU, her constant badgering about New York's high cost of living and dangerous neighborhoods brought out my toxic hostility during our phone calls. Now, with spring break approaching, graduation two months away and my parents' painful divorce signed, I could hear it in her voice on the phone. My 45-year-old mother, already incapable of letting her daughter go, was becoming desperate.

"Next week, when you're home for spring break, you can help me plan the garden for the new guest cottage. You're going to love it. It's got old gray cedar clapboards, flower boxes, two bedrooms, and an office overlooking a pine forest that would be perfect for writing."

"Mom, I've told you. I'm not moving back to Vermont after graduation; I'm staying in the city."

"Honey, you won't be in a dorm anymore. A writer cannot afford rent in New York City. You can live here rent free, and it's so close to Burlington. We can even subdivide the property so you could own it someday."

"Mom, why do you have to be so negative? I already have three friends that want to share an apartment. I'm making good money waiting tables nights and weekends so I can write during the day."

"You can write your stories anywhere; you don't have to be in New York. Your father brainwashed you to think it's the center of the universe. Well, it's not."

"That's a laugh. Dad was too busy with his professor friends. He took me to lunch at the stupid diner whenever he was feeling guilty."

"Awfully coincidental, you insisting on going to school in New York just like your father."

"You're not hearing me! I'm tired of Vermont. I don't want to live there. And I'm not a replacement for Dad."

"That's an awful thing to say. You can be a real bitch sometimes. You know that, Sher?"

"Mom, it's always been your way, driving me to school instead of letting me take the bus with my friends, picking out my clothes, dragging me to your church functions. And now that you and Dad have split, you want me to be your neighbor. Well, it's not happening. I'm twenty-one and I'm sick of it and I'm sick of quaint Vermont and its stupid craft beer. You're just going to have to do more volunteer work at the dog shelter to fill your time. I have other things I want to do with my life."

A week later, I landed at Burlington airport for my two week spring break. Mom was waiting for me in her rusting green 1962 Willy's pick-up truck. She greeted me with a long hug and a smug comment about how expensive flying home must have been. It was a five-minute drive to her new post-divorce house, a much smaller property than the beloved twenty-acre farmhouse we lived in for twenty years, far from Burlington. If anyone asked, she had downsized, but I knew the house with gardens near downtown Burlington was part of her calculus to lure her skeptical daughter back to Vermont. To me, it didn't matter if her new house was on Main Street, it was still centuries from New York City.

"The house needs some landscaping, and you can design whatever you want."

"Mom, it's your house. You should plant what you want. Besides, what do I know about designing gardens?"

"Sher, you've always loved flowers and gardening. You can plant all the zinnias you want. Anything."

"Mom, that was years ago. I have other interests."

"Sher, give it a chance. At least wait until you've seen it. It's so close to downtown and the university. You'll see."

My childhood fondness for gardening and obsession

with colorful flowers evidently imbued me with the skills of a landscape architect. And if my involvement in planning this garden caused me to reconsider Vermont as my home after college and filled the hole in her sad life, well, a mother can dream, can't she? She had hired a local nurseryman who was going to turn my girlhood dream garden into reality. After lunch, we'd drive over to meet him. During the next two weeks, Henry Laine made several visits to the house, and we had many conversations, some even about the garden.

ELLEN

She *had* to choose a college in New York. But that was her father talking. I knew he had been proselytizing her since high school when he'd pick her up from summer writing class and take her to the village diner for lunch. Cobb salad accompanied by dire warnings of missed life experiences if she chose to attend a college here in "the country," as if Vermont was some kind of disabled time machine stuck in its Transcendentalist past, its inhabitants unaware of any cultural development of the past fifty years. I'm sure he thrilled her with the intellectual awakenings of his college days in New York. The Associate Professor of Communications at the University of Vermont advising his prized pupil, with the added bonus of teaching me a lesson about the consequences of a rural lifestyle.

Our 1880 farmhouse on twenty acres was a brick of bucolic gold, but he could only complain that it was too heavy. The forty-minute drive to the university made socializing with his compatriots there difficult. He resented having to endure our small town's Memorial Day parades with our "bumpkin" town commissioner Arnold Floyd "smiling like an idiot" while driving the fire chief's shiny red 1959 Ford pickup down Elm Street. He'd plot his escape from the church basement during potluck dinners of homemade chili, potato salad, cornbread, and Bonnie Winslow's award-winning rhubarb cake, just to get back home to sip his bourbon and read the latest Steven Pinker book. Our big-hearted neighbors—dairy farmers, beekeepers, tradesmen—who joined us for Friday night fish fries at the local VFW post were "illiterate boors."

He destroyed our marriage to escape our Arcadian prison of clean air, virtuous community, and caring neighbors. But inflicting that cruelty wasn't enough. He had corrupted our daughter with slanders that trivialized not only my dream of a nourishing pastoral life for our family but my identity itself. In the divorce, Mitch took the cash, and I got the house, which I promptly sold to buy a smaller house a few minutes outside of Burlington. When he heard that, he became his vindictive self.

"On the edge of town! I guess you didn't need the cows and town picnics and the acres out in the middle of nowhere after all."

"Now that I'm on my own, I don't need that big house anymore."

"We could've sold it four years ago."

"I didn't want to sell it four years ago."

"Yeah, because I wanted to."

"You got what you wanted. You can live near your friends now."

"You're not fooling anyone. Sher isn't going to move into your cottage."

"Yes, thanks to you."

"I had nothing to do with it. She had her own plans. She hates you and your coddling. You're right about one thing— you're on your own. Get used to it."

I picked Sher up at the airport, choosing to forget her bitchiness on our phone call a week earlier. We arrived at the new house, unloaded her luggage and toured the guest cottage where Sher struggled to smile. I hoped it was the musty smell.

After lunch, we drove to Laine's Nursery. As a young girl, Sher enjoyed shopping at the garden stores. She'd spend hours planting and tending rows of flowers around our old farmhouse, insisting on zinnias in a rainbow of colors. I'd pick her up from school and she'd ask to ride in the bed of my pickup so she could see and hear and smell the wildflowers, streams, and pines as they traveled in the opposite direction. At home, she'd put on her flowered gardening gloves to deadhead her zinnias and test the soil for moisture and ask me with dire concern whether our fertilizer had the right amount of nitrogen.

I took the route that passed Sarah Tucker's apiary set on hilly acres filled with fragrant pines and a vociferous stream whose downhill surge danced over moss covered ledges. We drove across an old covered bridge whose wooden floorboards thwacked like a drum in double time under the weight of the truck and whose crimson color begged for autumn to begin. I was delighted that she had cell service on her phone.

I had met Henry Laine after moving into the new house. He was tall and slender, with thick white hair and a wide smile. Every part of his tanned and weathered 76-year-old face evoked the happiness of a life well-lived. Even the crow's feet at his temples made his soft blue eyes smile, a silent invitation to "stop by anytime," which I often did, bringing him his favorite cider donuts and chamomile tea. Henry's nephews managed most of the work around the nursery, leaving Henry to do what he enjoyed most: sharing his horticultural expertise with his customers.

In truth, Henry mostly enjoyed listening to his customers. But when he listened, he didn't do it like some of my ex-husband's aloof friends from the university who looked as though they were listening but were really just waiting for a chance to interrupt with their own ideas. Henry listened to understand. When he did speak, it was often to ask questions about you, earnest questions whose only purpose was to get to know you better. A person felt respected and safe in his company, and soon, we were talking about children, community, spouses, thoughts of the future and the past. Some of the thoughts I shared were more suited to a psychologist's office, but in that weathered, guileless, 76-year-old face, I hoped to find some heretofore elusive answers to my painful questions. It also seemed possible that Henry Laine was the sort of man who could induce some miraculous change of heart in my daughter.

HENRY

With landscape jobs, there's easy and there's hard. Ellen's plan seemed easy: she'd design a garden for the main house and her daughter would design one for the guest cottage. Of course, I had just gotten to know Ellen and hadn't met her daughter yet. What sounded like a simple plan would mutate into something more complicated, something better suited to a therapist. But people say I have a trustworthy face. They tell me their problems, their concerns, even their confessions. It would have been simpler to avoid getting involved in her family matters, but I always did want a family.

Ellen and I cherished our simple homes, our friends, our community, and the practice of treating every guest in our homes as though they were family. In her kitchen, overlooking a bare patch of black earth, she served me chamomile tea and freshly baked blueberry muffins on her grandmother's blue Delft china. She was undeterred by the dirt under my fingernails as she handed me an antique linen napkin. We sipped tea and talked about our favorite flowers while listening to a delicate Chopin nocturne playing on a turntable that looked as old as her Willy's pickup. The bare patch of dirt would make a lovely garden.

After our first meeting, I drove back to the nursery thinking of how she reminded me of Maxie. Not physically. Ellen was slight, with a down-turned smile, tawny hair, and round metal-rimmed glasses. Maxie's broad shoulders and black hair brought to mind the horse she hoped to own someday. When I would tell her that, she'd slap me on the back and roar with laughter. It was their congeniality and simplicity that could have made them sisters. Maxie dreamed of a modest house with a barn and a stream on a few acres of woods, with a Friesian horse to ride through the trees. We'd talk of filling the house with babies and letting the lullaby of the rushing stream put them to sleep. As the children grew, we'd add more horses. We'd ride together in the cold autumn wind until our faces shined pink. Back home, we'd sit by the fireplace under serape blankets drinking hot chocolate until we were warm. That was our dream. We just ran out of time.

Ellen and I enjoyed coffee and donuts at the town diner, ate her homemade carved chicken sandwiches for lunch behind my greenhouse, and not a single head in town turned with racy speculation. Our age difference, along with our unspoken proprieties, made it clear we were nothing more than friendly neighbors who shared a closeness and trust. Soon we were speaking openly about our lives, with welcome therapeutic effect. We talked about anger and dreams, about a selfish ex-husband, about disappointment and loneliness. We spoke profoundly about children, both the wished for and the unappreciative, and how a weathered 76-year-old face struggled to suppress an abiding sorrow for a long-dead wife.

Ellen was fascinated with my knowledge of horticulture, self-taught decades ago in our local library and in the dirt and peat of my father's cranberry bogs. For her garden, I imagined dogwoods (*Cornus sericea*), with their festive red twigs in winter, lining the stone path behind the main house and hosta (*Hosta lancifolia*) to trim the shaded walkways. Ellen was partial to rhododendron and had in mind a purple variety (*Ericaceae Rhododendron catawbiense*) for the space near her fir trees. She hadn't yet decided on the shade tree for the center of her sloping lawn near the stream. Under it, there would be picnics with friends and reunions with her large extended family.

Long ago, I read that orcas in the open sea swim hundreds of miles to distant places at speeds up to thirty-five miles per hour, but orcas in captivity, bound by the constrictive walls of their prison, never reach those speeds or those places, and as a result their dorsal fins droop downward in a sad signal of surrender.

It was the second meeting between Sher and me, a few days after she'd arrived home from school. She stopped by the nursery in her mom's truck. Sher was the same height as her mom, with the same down-turned smile and tawny hair. Everything else about her was unique. Ellen chose safe and predictable plants for the main house. Sher was more exotic, suggesting audacious plants as if her goal was to make the garden as challenging as possible to maintain. She asked about pots of Swamp Rose Mallow (*Hibiscus moscheutos*), a tropical plant that was tolerant to cold, Seven Sons (*Heptacodium miconionides*), a spectacular and fragrant flowering shrub native to China, and, to frame the entranceway, enchanting pink oleanders (*Nerium oleander*). When I suggested simple, colorful zinnias for the window boxes, Sher grinned.

"What else did my mother tell you about me?"

I chuckled at her quick wit. "She told me how much you love flowers, especially zinnias, that's all."

"No offense, but my flower obsession ended ten years ago."

"That's not possible, everyone loves flowers."

She smiled. "You sound like a guy who owns a nursery."

I laughed at that one. "I hear you're a writer. Thoreau did some pretty good writing in a place like this."

"Ah, I see. This isn't going to be just about flowers and trees, is it? Look, Mr. Laine—"

"Please, call me Henry."

"Henry, it's a beautiful cottage, really, but this life is not for me, if you know what I mean."

"Yes, I think I do. You have a sparkle in your eye. I'm sure there are big things in your future. I just think your mom is looking forward to working on the garden with you and hoping you'll put your own touch on it."

"She's looking forward to more than me just working on it now that she and my dad got divorced. I told her, the country life isn't for me, but she's hanging on, hoping. She's sort of been hanging on me my whole life, but she's going to have to deal with her situation on her own."

I gave her a sympathetic smile. "I think your involvement will do a great deal to lift her spirits."

"Yeah, and if you can convince me to move into that cottage, she'll throw a party and you'll be the guest of honor."

Now we both laughed out loud.

"Who did you get your sense of humor from?" I asked.

"Well, you know my mom—she's as funny as a mortician. My dad, he's never been a humorous person either. To be honest, he doesn't like living out here. He's always enjoyed being around his professor friends more than being home with us. It kind of sucks, but that's him."

"Yes, that does suck. I suppose you're right about the cottage. Young people need to do their own thing. But I can understand why your mom wants to have you close by. I know if I had kids, I'd want to see them every day."

"Were you ever married?"

"I was, a long time ago, but Maxie got sick before we ever had a chance to get going."

"I'm sorry."

"It's funny, you and your mom want such different lives, yet both of you remind me of Maxie. She was a homebody like your mom. When we were young, she was content to spend Saturday nights with me, a bonfire, and sixpack of beer. On summer days, she'd visit our 85-year-old widowed neighbor, Mrs. Turnbull. They'd sit in her garden, and Maxie would listen to her go on and on about her secret to growing her 'Grateful Heart' tea roses (*Rosa x hybrida*) that lined her white picket fence. But then, Maxie also had an adventurous side, like you. I remember her driving us to Smuggler's Notch for my surprise birthday gift, an afternoon of ziplining down the mountain."

"C'mon, you were young. That's not so adventurous."

"It is if you're afraid of heights like she was. But she saw some kids doing it and thought what the hell. Another time I'd found her on her computer taking French lessons. Never said a word, just started taking lessons. When I asked her about it, she said the language sounded like beautiful poetry. ... I'm sorry ... this always gets me ..."

"Please, don't apologize."

"She said she wanted to understand the poem."

"How sweet."

"She was. Meeting you and your mom has brought it all back, wondering what my life with Maxie would've been like, what our kids would have been like. I've always had a vision of that, but I guess it could've turned out a million different ways."

"I'm sorry you never had a chance for a family. You sound like you'd be a pretty good father. And you're right, you never know how things will turn out. Things were wonderful when I was a kid, we did things together as a family. We'd hike around the twenty acres and put our feet in the streams on hot summer days. All of us, even Dad, were in awe watching our neighbor Mr. Davis milk his cows. Toasting marshmallows around a fire was a family event, me with chocolate milk, Mom with a glass of wine, and Dad with his bourbon. Over time, we did those things less and less, until it all fell apart, Mom and Dad, us. I guess people change. I used to love it here, but now, it's just not for me. I want to write my book in my own place."

"Right. Someplace without walls, where you can go far and fast."

"Yes."

The last load of mulch was spread, and it was done. What a strange trick of fate that a man like me who treasured the soil, flowers, sunshine, all timeless things of purity, would be drawn in by this family for whom toxic words and actions had become the weapons of choice to poison the thing in themselves that was surely innocent and pure long ago. And now, it was only natural that these two women would invite poison into their garden, lovely, fragrant poison, *Ericaceae Rhododendron catawbiense* and *Nerium oleanders*. And it was only natural in the presence of such toxins, that a gardener would discover seeds of doubt that his own cherished, restorative, sustaining dreams of pure things like black horses, shining pink faces, blankets, and lullabies, were ever possible.

At the center of the sloping lawn near the stream was the new tree. It was only sixteen feet tall but would grow to sixty, providing many years of shade for Ellen's family reunions.

She chose Autumn Blaze (*Sapindaceae Acer x freemanii*), a neat and uncomplicated red maple variety that drops no seeds, assuring it would stand alone without offspring for as long as it lived.

REUNION

DEDE was in the kitchen making coffee on a Saturday morning in April when I saw the email on my phone. *You're invited. Please join us on Saturday, October 17, 2015, in Dobbs Ferry, New York, for the Ten Year Reunion of Horace Greeley High School's Class of 2005.* But what I read was: *You're invited. Please join us for an evening explaining to people you haven't seen in ten years how you managed to fuck up your life, your big plan, the plan you described to everyone back in high school.* I had six months to think about whether I'd go or not, but what I was thinking of at that moment was the famous boxer who said, "Everybody's got a plan until they get punched in the face."

Dede had a plan too. Three years earlier, she had left her hometown of Carbonville, Pennsylvania, for New York City, or as close to it as she could afford, which turned out to be my town: Bloomfield, New Jersey. She rented a tiny studio apartment four blocks from mine and enrolled in the tattooing program on the second floor of the Tools & Arts Trade School on Broad Street. She'd tell me later that when the smell of ink mixed with gasoline fumes from the mechanic's class in the garage below, it gave her something freakishly close to a two-beer buzz. At night, she was everyone's favorite bartender at the Bow 'n Stern, a local beer and burger joint. It was a temporary gig until she could open her own tattoo shop. She pocketed big tips from the patrons by rocking out with them on air guitar to AC/DC songs and by laughing at their bad jokes, always with an eye on that ink shop. But she was looking for a different payback besides tips when she poured buyback drinks for Mr. Vronsky, the balding, sixty-ish small-business loan manager at the local Citibank branch.

It was that summer, in 2012, when we met. She'd been in Bloomfield only a few weeks. At five o'clock, I left work at the Auto Spot store and headed for the Bow 'n Stern for a burger at the bar."

"Can I get you something to drink?" she asked.

"I'm not sure what I want."

"Let me help you out. Here's a beer list, cocktails and wine on the back. My name's Dede. Take your time, but we close at midnight." She raised her eyebrows and gave me a tight-lipped smile.

"Midnight. I'll make it quick then. A Bud."

Two months later, with a flirtatious expression and a few blinks of her big brown eyes, she convinced her landlord to let her out of her lease so she could move in with me above Wu Hop's Chinese restaurant. We were two small, wiry, flat-chested strays looking for a destination. I liked her big brown eyes, too, and her button nose, her long, black hair in a shag cut, the dark eyeliner and violet lipstick. She was a cute badass in her heavy-metal muscle shirts that exposed not muscles but a jungle of tattoos. The most prominent was on her right shoulder painted with bold block letters in rainbow colors that read: *Dream Big*. She liked to run her hands through my long blond hair and was impressed by the way I didn't take any crap from people, which was funny because she would never have said that if she had known me in high school. But the thing we liked most about each other, maybe needed is a better word, is that we both understood anger.

Growing up in Carbonville, the gray skies, knee-high weeds, smoke from the steel mills, and the empty beer cans around her dad's double-wide in the Furnace Creek Trailer Park made it easy, even enjoyable, for Dede to slam the door and rattle the windows when she'd leave for her job stamping prices on the canned peas and beef jerky in the stockroom at Muncy's Village Store. On the day she came home with her first tattoo, her dad put down his bottle of Wild Turkey and asked with a contemptible grin that came easily to him, "What the hell is that? *Dream Big*. Hell, you dreamin' to marry the Muncy boy and become what, head cashier? Woohoo! Cause then we could buy a big mansion with a swimmin' pool."

"You have no idea what my dreams are cause you never asked. But I'll tell you one thing, they sure aren't gonna happen for me here."

Dede had learned not to say too much when her dad had a bottle, which was most days. A month later she sold the gold necklace her mom had given her before she died, emptied her savings account, said an uncontested goodbye to her dad, and climbed on a bus that kicked up stale Carbonville dust and headed for New York.

My shit goes back to Greeley High. I was too small and uncoordinated to play on any sports teams and my grades were just mediocre, so I came and went without much notice. Although, a couple of the less popular girls seemed to like something about me. Maybe it was my quiet, shy nature, or my longish blond hair, or my optimistic attitude and smile that drew their interest. Or, it might have been the old Civic hatchback that I fixed up, complete with a custom sound system blasting Nirvana or Zeppelin, that drew their interest. Still, no quality I possessed could overcome the intimidation I felt at school. The smart kids, the athletes, the motorheads, and of course, the girls, even the ones who let me drive them home in the Civic, sensed my sheepish anxiety, and they had their fun at my expense. I had nothing going for myself beside that jalopy, so I made up a future, my big plan for the future. Soon, I believed it myself. How I was going to be the first one in my family to go to college. How I'd get a big job in computer tech. How I'd wear sharp clothes and live in the cool part of downtown Manhattan. That was my plan, until senior year anyway, when I was introduced to Majestic Ventures LLC.

When Dede first moved in with me, we both knew when to talk about the anger that lived inside us and when to shut up and let the anger fly into things and break them into a million pieces, as if releasing the rage was a therapy, an antibiotic that needed to run its course. Frustration and anger were always close by in both of us, just under the surface waiting for an excuse to be set free. Sometimes ordinary aggravations would set us off, like a bungled pizza delivery or a customer's complaint because I sold him the wrong intake gasket. Stuff like that might cause a low grade fever of cursing and slamming things down on the table. But sometimes it was heavier stuff, like being asked if the scar camouflaged by a tattoo was a cigarette burn or a dismal memory made real again by an unwelcome Saturday morning email. Then the anger was different, more subtle, poisonous, difficult to erase and move beyond.

But just because you live with someone for three years doesn't mean you both move past your pain toward some kind of happiness at the same speed, or that you progress at all. The promise of her ink shop was enough for Dede. My contentment was still hanging out there somewhere in the murk, stubbornly beyond my reach. I wasn't even sure of what I was reaching for. I learned it was possible to live with someone and still feel alone and that loneliness can make a person think fucked-up things. It didn't matter that my vindictiveness was directed at someone whose only sin was trying move toward happiness by evicting her anger and filling the void with self-control and self-awareness and self-love, all of which might someday take up residence in me as well. It was perversely satisfying to see her progress slowed when she didn't get the expected raise at the Bow 'n Stern, when she received a lower than expected grade in her tattoo class, even when her hand-wash-only sweater was accidently tossed in the washer. How small and spiteful and selfish it was to find such joy in throwing a rock at her car as it traveled on her road to happiness, passing me by as I thumbed a ride. This was the cost I imposed on Dede for the sin of leaving me behind.

Dede brought me a cup of coffee as I stared at the email on my phone. I was in a fog repeating the word *reunion* over and over in my head until that weird thing happens where suddenly the word sounds like gibberish. *Reunion. Re-union. Re-u-nion.*

I was startled by her voice over my shoulder, "Wow, your ten-year reunion. Cool."

"I'm not going."

"Why not?"

"I'm just not into it."

"Why?"

"Cause I don't give a shit about the people from high school."

"What about Kent and Benny?"

"Yeah, it'd be nice to see them, but still, I'm not going."

"Can you tell me why?"

"Cause it's a fucking competition, that's why."

"Seriously! Are you talking about the college thing?"

"Yes, okay. I really don't want to go through it with all those assholes."

"Hey babe, I get it that your embarrassed about what happened, but—"

"I'm not embarrassed, I just don't want to go."

"That was ten years ago. Things didn't turn out the way you planned, so what. It wasn't your fault. I think you should forget all that and go to the reunion."

"I'm not going. And why do you care if I go or not?"

"I know you don't want to hear this again, but it'd be a good chance to make some new connections—"

"Oh fuck. This again?"

"You said it yourself; you need to make a move. The reunion could be a good place to meet old friends who might be able to hook you up with a new job."

"Yeah, right. Like any of them give a shit about me."

She lit a cigarette and exhaled sideways through violet lips that she scrunched way over to the side of her face. Whenever she did that, it meant she had some big, important comment to make so I'd better listen.

"What if someone from your class owns a company or has some big job in the city. If they know you're looking to make a change . . . you never know."

"Yeah, the guy who bragged about becoming a computer star in the city is gonna explain how his big plan crashed and burned and then panhandle for a job."

"Vince, no one's gonna remember what you said ten years ago. You were just a high school kid talking shit."

"I'd look like an idiot begging for help. Fuck that."

"Look, do you want to get your life in gear or not?"

"Oh, like this is your area of expertise. The bigshot tattoo artist is giving me tips on how to be successful."

"Hey, at least I set a goal. I have half the money I need to open my own shop. So you can shit on it all you want, but it's gonna happen."

"And your big tattoo license, from that stupid trade school that you had to hang on the wall with the fancy lettering like it's a real diploma."

"I worked hard for that, Vince. Why shouldn't I hang it up?"

"I know exactly why you hung it up, right by the front door."

"Vince, this isn't about me. I'm trying to help you."

"Yeah, well, I don't want your help cause I'm not going."

Brooke Goodwin sat next to me in English class. She was two inches taller than me and looked like a supermodel. In class she'd start conversations like we were real friends. So, after a few weeks I worked up the courage to ask Supermodel to go across the street for a slice of pizza at the Half Moon. She looked at me like I had asked her to do my homework for me, then she smiled and started laughing. She didn't say a word, she just laughed. See, there was no risk for her to talk to the ordinary kid sitting next to her in class because that didn't mean she was really interested in me, it was just the luck of the seating chart. But in the hallway, she'd pretend she didn't know me because to show any interest there meant we were actual friends, or worse, that she liked me, and she wasn't about to let anyone think that.

"Look, do you want to rent this shoebox apartment above this smelly restaurant for the rest of your life? Well, I don't. C'mon Vince, go to the reunion, smile, be friendly."

In my junior year, Marty Valent, one of the assholes on the football team, grabbed me by the shirt and bench-pressed me in front of all the cheerleaders. I laughed like I was in on the gag. The girls picked up the change that fell out of my pockets and giggled as they handed it to me. "Here's your milk money, Vincent."

"How about if I go to the reunion with you? I'll wear my smokin' hot black mini dress. You can wear your navy suit with that red tie. You'll look super successful with a hot girlfriend."

"Yeah, Dede, a successful 28-year-old clerk in an auto parts store."

"Just tell them you're the manager. You run the place when your boss is out, don't you?"

Before an exam in trig class, I asked Hart to help me with an equation. He went through it so quickly that I got more confused. He knew I was still confused, but he smiled and said, "See, easy, right?" One day in the cafeteria I told him about my plan, and in front of everyone, he looked through his horned-rimmed glasses and said, "You're too indolent to succeed in college." He knew I had no idea what indolent meant.

"Like I need to see those jerks at a reunion. And you want me to wear my crappy, 10-year-old navy blue suit that my dad bought for me. What a joke, Dede. I could've had an apartment in Manhattan with a closet full of Italian suits."

* * *

Hattie's Bar near the Dobbs Ferry train station was a local establishment inhabited by an unlikely mix of gritty locals in greasy shirts driving pickup trucks and soft executives in starched collars fresh off the Metro-North commuter train. At Hattie's, there were no lines of separation between the gritty and the starched. Each had something the other wanted, a job without 24/7 pressure or a career with big money that bought big things. For years, Carson Quigley's manicured hands and Dad's blue shirt with "DAVE" sewn on its chest, would meet at Hattie's after work. Quigley would hop off the train from his advertising job in Manhattan, and Dad would stop in after his shift at the post office. They'd drink beer and watch ball games with some of the regulars. A few times a year, they'd go to Yonkers Raceway to bet on the trotters.

One late afternoon in March of my junior year in high school, Dad and I were sitting in a booth in the back room waiting for our burgers when Quigley walked in.

"I'll be right back," Dad said. At the bar, he clapped Quigley on the shoulder, "Hey, Cars."

"Whoa, the mailman's here. No bills please," Carson shouted.

Dad felt the lapel of Quigley's charcoal pinstripe suit between his thumb and index finger. As Quigley spoke to the bartender, I could see Dad eyeing that impeccably tailored suit from top to bottom, still rubbing invisible wool between his fingers.

"Heineken, Fran. You want one, Dave, or are you still on duty?" Quigley punched the American flag on Dad's shoulder.

"No, thanks." Dad pointed to me in our booth. "I'm havin' a burger with Vince."

Quigley looked my way and waved.

"Nice suit, Cars. New?"

"Yeah, you know, you have to look the part to get ahead. Hey, just be happy you don't have to wear a suit every day. They cost a fortune."

"You kiddin'? Being all knotted up in a suit and tie every day would drive me nuts. What kind of wool is it?"

Quigley exposed the label inside the jacket. "One hundred percent *Lana Italia*. That's Italian for wool, fine Italian worsted wool, my friend." Dad was still staring at that label when Quigley pulled a photograph out of his pocket. "Dave, check this out."

"A building?"

"Eight-floor apartment building near Wilmington, Delaware. I'm a part owner of it."

"You're movin' to Delaware?"

"No, dummy, it's an investment. I bought shares in a company that buys old beat-up buildings, fixes them up, and sells them or rents them out. And I get a share of the profits."

"No shit. How long have you been doin' that?"

"I bought my shares in this building three months ago. I got my second check yesterday."

"How much?"

"Four hundred."

"How much did you invest?"

"Eight thousand. They can't guarantee how big the ROI will be, but judging from what the vice president of sales and a few other investors told me, I figure about 18 percent annual return, so I'll double my investment in about four years. The Rule of Seventy-Two my friend."

"What's that?"

"Divide seventy-two by the rate of return, and it tells you how long it will take to double your money. Seventy-two divided by eighteen means I'll double my money in four years. All the big investment bankers know about it."

"Right, right, I read about that. The Rule of Seven and—"

"Not seven, seventy-two. I'm going to make another investment next month for an office building in Florida. This company's got properties all over the East Coast. And, if I bring in other investors, I get a small piece of their profits too. It's a sweet deal with great returns and very little risk. This is a great way to get in on the real estate boom. Not that I'm trying to sell you on it, but if you're interested, I can set up a meeting in the city with them."

"You have any information about the company? You know, like how long they've been in business, details of how it works, you know, to research? I might be interested. That is, you know, if the *arro-eye* is good."

"Sure, tomorrow after work. I'll bring their brochures. You can even talk to their other investors."

"Don't get me wrong—my job at the Postal Service is great. Tons of seniority and the pension's awesome, but I'm always lookin' out for good investments."

"Yeah, you should think about this one. It could change your life."

"Okay, thanks, Cars. I'll see you tomorrow."

Dad walked back to our booth smiling as he swiped his hands together like two cymbals glancing off one another, and I heard him say something about some kind of rule.

"Whadja say, Dad?"

He was still grinning, "Oh, nothin.'"

A few weeks later, Dad invested five thousand dollars for a share of an apartment building in North Carolina, and when he got his first check, he bought a bottle of champagne for his buddies at the bar.

"Fran, how do you pronounce it?"

"Voov Click-kwa. It's French."

"California champagne is nice, but there's nothing like the French."

"Dave, if it's from California, it's called sparkling wine."

"Yeah, yeah, same difference. Hey, is that house up on Ridge still for sale?"

"The big one with the pool? Yeah, I think so."

"I might go take a look at it."

"You buyin' a house?"

"Thinkin' about it."

"Gotta be a pretty steep price tag on that place. Must be four thousand square feet."

"I'm tired of paying rent. And it would be a great investment."

"Yeah, but it's a lot of house for just you and Vince."

"You know the old saying: you can't take it with you. Plus, I could throw one helluva pool party for the guys."

For months, the checks rolled in. In September, Quigley took a second mortgage on his house and Dad nearly emptied his savings account. They bought into an outdoor mall in Miami. The next week, Dad toured that house on Ridge and test drove the car of his dreams, a red Ford Thunderbird convertible. I saw him shopping online for a Rolex, and he told me to start applying to colleges. He even asked me if I thought I could get into the Ivy League.

Then, October came, but their checks didn't. Frantic texts to the vice president were ghosted, and calls to the company were answered with a robotic voice saying, "That number has been disconnected." Dad and Quigley gave descriptions and looked at mug shots, but the detectives said there wasn't much chance that they'd find the guys. All that was left of Majestic Ventures LLC was the sign on the door. *Majestic Ventures.* How pathetic was that. I threw the applications in the trash. Dad, too embarrassed to show his face at Hattie's, started drinking at home, alone.

* * *

"Give me the reunion date and I'll put it on my calendar in case you change your mind and you want me to come with you."

"Just drop it, Dede. I'm not going to the fucking reunion."

"Suit yourself." She smiled and blew smoke out of the side of her face.

I put my phone in my pocket. *Reunion, re-union, re-u-nion.* "Dede, I'm driving over to Dobbs Ferry. Max has a little league game at two o'clock."

"Whoa! What are you talking about?"

"I'm going to his game."

"Just like that? Outta the blue, you're going to see Max? You can't do that Vince."

"Yes, I can."

"No, you *can't*. Stop Vince. Wait! You can't just show up after ten years. You're not allowed—"

"I can do whatever I want."

"How do you know he has a ball game? Did you talk to her?"

"Kent sends me her posts about him on Facebook."

"This is a bad idea, Vince."

"So what. What's one more bad idea?"

* * *

Charlotte Boine and her parents piled into their Chevy Venture and left Bluffton, Indiana, in September 2005 for a new life in Dobbs Ferry, New York. I met her at the town's Labor Day parade on Ashford Avenue, staring at her long auburn hair and shapely, innocent lips that let you see her cloud white teeth even when she wasn't smiling.

She was six feet away, looking in my direction, when she spoke. "Will there be fireworks after the parade? In Bluffton, we always had fireworks."

It took a minute before I realized that she was talking to me. She laughed at my confusion in the friendliest way. Her wide smile melted my nervousness, and she repeated her question.

"Uh, yes. Once it gets dark, they do fireworks at the ball field on the other side of town."

"Hi, I'm Charlotte."

"Hi, I'm Vincent. Where's Bluffton?"

"Indiana. We moved here for my father's new job. Six hundred and seventy-two miles. Gosh, I don't know what was worse, the car ride or unpacking our stuff. Our house is on Overlook Road."

"I live in the Gardens, that way, on Broadway. Been here my whole life."

"Bluffton was nice, but really small. I graduated in June from Bluffton High and there were only twenty-five kids in my class."

"I graduated in June, too, from Greeley. Must have been hundreds of kids at graduation. Are you going to college?"

"No, I'm doing a year of mission work with our new church here, Calvary Methodist. When I'm finished, I'll go to college, probably around here. Mom and Dad want me to stay close to home. How about you?"

"I'm taking a year off too. I figured I'd get a job and save some money first." I didn't want to look into her eyes while telling that lie, so I looked at the sky.

"Hey," she said, "did I see a Baskin Robbins around here? Do you want to get some ice cream?"

"Sure, it's right up the street."

"Are you staying for the fireworks?"

"Yeah, they usually start around nine thirty."

"If you want, I can drive us to the ball field."

"You have a car?"

"Uh huh. A convertible."

"My dad would kill for a convertible."

"My dad bought it for me. He felt bad about taking me away from my friends in Bluffton. But you know Vincent, I already like it here in Dobbs Ferry."

"You do?"

"Yes. It's pretty here. I mean, you have so many hills. Bluffton is flat as a lake. Let's get some ice cream."

Later, with the top down in her red Ford Mustang convertible, she drove us to the ball field. There was a big crowd, and we sat together on the outfield grass. The sky was still light, but Charlotte Boine had already lit the fuse on our own fireworks.

A week later we were skimming stones by the lake when the subject of college came up again.

"Vincent, are you getting a job so you can pay for college?"

She saw the pain in my face as I picked up a stone and walked toward the lake. Glaring at the ripples on the water, I said, "I'm not going to college."

She squinted with confusion, "But you said you wanted to save money first."

"I know I said that but . . . I'm not going to college."

"Is it because of the money?"

"Yes."

"Can your dad help?"

I skimmed the stone so hard it nearly made it to the other side of the lake, "Charlotte, I was going to apply for school, but my dad . . . well, he had the money . . . he was going to pay for it . . . it's so stupid!"

"What happened?"

"He lost the money to some con men."

I took a deep, shuddering breath and told her about Majestic Ventures. How one mistake, one bad decision ruined everything.

"He told everyone he loved his job, but I knew he hated it. He tried to hide it, but if you saw him around the Manhattan crowd at Hattie's, you would've seen it too. He was a different person around them."

"Were you angry at him for losing your tuition money?"

I hesitated as I measured my options. Finally, I answered, "No."

"Good for you. Forgiveness is hard, but it's always best."

A single, tiny word—no. How easy it was to lie just to be loved. She gave me an approving smile, reached for my hand, and leaned toward me. It was the first kiss for both of us, and it was as awkward and tender and electrifying as our dreams had promised.

We cruised through the month of September in her Mustang. At night, after a movie or an ice cream, Charlotte would drop me off a block away from my house so Dad wouldn't see her convertible. I wanted to tell her how I felt about her, hoping she felt the same way, but I thought maybe she just felt sorry for me after hearing my sad story. Then, on a Friday night, with the top down and the wind whipping at us, Charlotte tossed her hair back with a laugh, drove past the woods to a clearing behind the ball field and turned off the motor. She held my face in her slender hands and kissed me. She didn't say a word, she just kissed me. We fell into the back seat, she on me, we fumbled with zippers and buttons, and I held her hips and looked up to see the waving branches of oak trees surrounding us and Charlotte's smiling face and long brown hair shifting forward and back in the moonlight, first covering the moon, then uncovering it, then covering it again, and again, and again, and again. After that night, whenever we drove with the top down, the reflection in the windshield was filled with tossed hair, waving branches, and moonlight.

Two months later in the front seat of her Mustang, I offered to use my savings to pay for an abortion. I told her I would stay by her side every minute. But that Bible in her parents' living room wasn't some decorative accent like a bouquet of plastic flowers and her father's question weeks earlier about what church I attended wasn't bogus small talk and when I answered him by saying I didn't attend church, his disappointment—well, that wasn't fake either.

Charlotte turned the motor off and said an abortion wasn't possible. She was going to have the baby, and she asked if I would marry her. She had already spoken with her parents, and despite their questionable opinion of me, they, too, thought we should get married. We were only eighteen, and I wanted to be with her all the time. I was sure that meant I was in love with her, and I told her so. What I wasn't sure of was whether her asking me to get married was the same as her saying I love you. Then, she kissed me softly; she didn't say a word, she just kissed me. I said yes, I'd marry her. But this time there was no moonlight.

"Vince, why not give the baby up for adoption?"

"We both want to get married and keep the baby."

"Is she pressuring you?

"No, I love her, Dad, and we want to get married."

"You're only eighteen, you're not ready for this."

"I've grown up a lot in the last year."

"You're both too young. And, if you keep that baby, you'll blow your chance to go to college."

Suddenly, I wanted to tear out his guts. The arsonist of my college plan was warning me about the dangers of fire.

"Oh, I should give up Charlotte and the baby, put myself in hock up to my ass, and spend years paying off college loans, just to bail you out of your guilt? That's not happening, Dad."

Dad's efforts to win over Mr. and Mrs. Boine on the merits of adoption had failed. We left for Bluffton on a frigid Thursday morning in December with stops in Chicago and Fort Wayne. We were married on Saturday in the Bethel Zion Methodist church. It was a small, rushed, family ceremony intended to minimize any potential embarrassment. No one asked why I had no family at the ceremony.

Max was born in Dobbs Ferry the following summer. Mr. Boine bought a small apartment for us to live in. We were married, so, legally, it probably didn't matter, but the message was clear when I saw that the only name on the deed was Charlotte's. She skipped her year of volunteer work and enrolled part time at Mercy College while her mother took care of the baby. I took a job with the sanitation department riding the back of a garbage truck.

I've read that it isn't unusual for new parents to become unnerved by an infant's prolonged crying. Not the routine cries of hunger or teething that can be calmed easily with milk or medication—I'm talking about a siren of wailing. Insistent. Persistent. Cries that, at first, are ignored hoping they'll result, eventually, in sleep, but do not. Wails that pause only to allow air to be sucked into tiny Herculean lungs before they resume. Shrieks that ignored my cradling hug and attempts to calm and became an unbearable, audible ice pick that pierced my brain.

I saw it after his head hit the inside rail of the crib. The force of the impact left a small reddish bruise on his forehead that multiplied his deafening screams and would later turn to a purple lump. I lurched out of the room slamming the door behind me. From the living room, Max's ghastly and merciless cries were muffled but still managed to drown out my own sobs as I caught sight of Charlotte's new Bible on the bookshelf and then Charlotte herself as she walked through the front door.

"What's wrong? Vincent, don't you hear him?"

She ran to Max's room, and I followed. "He won't stop crying. I tried everything but I couldn't—"

"Vince, you can't leave him alone when he's crying like this." She lifted him from his crib and held him close. "Shhh, Max, Mama's here, shhh." Then, "What happened to his head?"

"I don't know, he must've banged it against the crib."

I should have just told her what happened, apologized, and begged for forgiveness. A serious lapse of judgment. Two, if you count lying about it. I'd forgotten about the video camera in Max's room. That ended the mystery. After she settled Max to sleep in his bassinette, she watched the video. Her eyes filled with a fury that accused me of the most inexcusable of sins.

"Vincent. How could you?"

Now it was Charlotte who was crying. She confronted me with an anger I had never seen before.

"How could you do that to your own baby?"

"He wouldn't stop screaming. I snapped. I don't know—"

"What kind of a person would do that? How can I ever trust you with him again? My father was right."

Now, the anger that allowed me to do such a despicable

thing to my own child emerged again in a volatile burst. Bottled up for years, my anger, now mixed with shame and desperation, spewed out at all of them: hateful classmates, scam artists, fathers, both the gullible and the righteous. Even the mother of my own son wasn't spared. I grabbed Charlotte's wrists and pushed her against the wall.

"Don't tell your father."

"Let go of me. Vincent, you're hurting me. Let go!"

"I'm serious, if you tell him or anyone, you'll be sorry."

She kneed my groin and I fell backward to the floor. Charlotte grabbed the bassinette. "Stay away from us!"

She put Max in his car seat, ran out the door and drove away.

Forgiveness, even for the Boines, was indeed hard, too hard. The divorce papers were signed a month later. The incident wouldn't be reported if I agreed to give up custody of Max and make no contact with Charlotte or Max until he was eighteen years old. I quit my job and moved across the river to New Jersey, never saying a proper goodbye.

* * *

The oak trees surrounding the Dobbs Ferry ball field were still there, filled now with bittersweet memories. I stood hidden beyond the left-field fence under the distant memory of waving branches that, today, blocked the sunlight. A white van painted with large lettering that read Sam Brock HVAC pulled into the parking lot nearby. Sam Brock got out wearing navy blue overalls and a ball cap with a curved bill and a logo on the front. He walked to the stands near the infield and kissed Charlotte and the two young girls sitting next to her. Charlotte was wearing a yellow sundress; Sam, jeans and his company's HVAC ball cap; his daughters, colorful overalls; and Max was warming up on the infield in his pinstriped uniform with ASTROS embroidered on the front. He had longish blond hair and a constant smile. His thin frame bounced up and down as he clowned in the dirt with his teammates. My friends, still connected to Charlotte, had told me he was a happy and popular kid, and it showed in the Brock family Facebook photos they shared with me over the years. But this wasn't a photograph. They talked, laughed, hugged.

When I had arrived at the field, my plan was to approach Charlotte, but seeing them together, I decided that having wrecked one family already, I couldn't wreck another. That's what they were, a family. Imposing myself on them now would just extend the damage I'd caused. Max would eventually have questions. He'd want to know what happened. He'd be confused, and wonder *what if*, just as I had since the days I threw my college applications in the trash and my infant son against his crib.

One of the girls shouted toward second base where Max was standing. He ran to meet Sam near the dugout. Sam spoke to him. Max shook his head up and down. They hugged each other, and Max ran back onto the field. Later, I would try to add this scene to my file of Facebook images— 5-year-old Max's first day of school, Halloween in a cowboy costume, a birthday party with candle flames turned to smoke, tearing Christmas wrapping off a train set, and now this, a little league ball game thick with love and encouragement . . . from his father.

I watched three innings and walked back to my car for the ride home. I looked at myself in the rearview mirror, but I already knew what was behind me. I wanted to see the future. I wanted to know if the questions and the confusion and the truth awaiting my son would be dark enough to transform his happiness to anger.

In the distance, the George Washington Bridge was silent as I drove south on the Henry Hudson Parkway, which hugged the river of the same name. As I crossed the bridge toward home, I took notice of the river's current, also silent, but visible, undeterred, insistent on moving forward.

I walked into our apartment just before dinner time. Dede watched me from the sofa and finally asked, "So, did you see him?"

"Uh huh."

"What did you do?"

"Nothing. I just watched him play from behind the trees."

"So, you didn't talk to anyone?"

"No. Her husband was there, too, with their two other kids. He looked like a nice guy and Max looked . . . like . . . every other kid playing ball with his parents watching from the stands."

"Are you okay, babe?"

"Yeah, I feel pretty good, actually."

She crossed the room and wrapped her arms around my neck and kissed me, "Good, I'm glad."

"I didn't stop for anything to eat. How about we walk over to Carlo's for a slice?"

"Sounds great, let's go."

When we arrived at Carlo's, we stopped to read an advertisement in the window for the Tools & Arts Trade School announcing their fall class offerings. I pulled out my phone and took a picture of it.

THE KINDNESS OF THE WIND

NONE of us kids wanted to move out of the Bronx, and we all had our reasons. I was eleven, Ronnie a year older. He liked the bedroom we shared. I liked the view of the Richmond Avenue El from our terrace on the fourth floor. I even liked the screech of the D train. Theo and J.J. were in high school and had girlfriends who lived on Richmond Avenue. They were furious when they heard about it. We all worried that there wouldn't be stickball games or egg creams in the country. Dad said we were only moving to the suburbs a few miles away, but for us in 1970, any place with houses and grass was *the country*. But even if all four of us had gotten on our knees and lit a candle at St. Mary's, it wouldn't have changed Dad's decision after what happened on that morning in June underneath the El on Richmond Avenue.

The round metal stools were permanently fastened to the floor near the counter. Behind the counter, Moe would make chocolate egg creams while I gambled my allowance praying for a Mickey Mantle in pack after pack of Topps baseball cards, the kind with a stick of bubble gum inside. Moe's candy store, a few blocks from Richmond on the corner of Belmont Avenue and 187th Street in the Bronx, is gone now. So are the cars with big chrome bumpers and parking meters that took dimes. Some things are still there, but the passing of fifty-two years warps memories. St. Mary's Church, Richmond Avenue, the El tracks above it, and even the D train that still thundered through all looked smaller than when I was eleven years old. It was the same with the lawns, houses, and streets in the Yonkers neighborhood we moved to in the summer of 1970. Everything was smaller except the trees, which the passage of time, like our ability to extract truth from the world, made larger. Recalling all the events of that time, it's not surprising that what I remember most about my new neighborhood is that all the houses were the same, except for their color.

It was the first day of September, and Mom had taken Ronnie and me to see our new house before the movers arrived. She said it was a three-bedroom colonial with white aluminum siding on a half-acre. We didn't see any stickball games being played on the streets, but there was a blue ping-pong table in the basement and a flat, sun-filled backyard of grass, perfect for football games. There was even a small doggie door leading to the yard, which made getting a dog seem like a real possibility. Dad arrived as the movers were finishing up. He walked through the house to make sure everything was in order. Then, he carried a big box and some tools to the far corner of our backyard. He set the box down near two large maple trees about twelve feet apart. I don't ever remember seeing Dad smile the way he did as he took the first swing in that hammock.

That Saturday, I swayed in the hammock and listened to Mom laugh as she brought drinks to the patio. Dad popped open another Ballantine beer and placed burgers over the glowing gray coals of our new grill. In social studies class at St. Mary's, Sister Agnes had taught us about the American Dream. I wasn't sure what it meant then but watching Mom and Dad from the hammock on that lazy Saturday afternoon, I began to understand.

It was three days until the start of school. Dad never told us why we wouldn't be attending parochial school anymore, but I had once overheard him tell Mom that the public schools out here were good and free. In the first week of school, I met Nicky, Simon, and Andy. They all lived on my street, and after school the four of us would ride our bikes to the woods behind the firehouse and then stop to cool off in Korvette's Department Store before getting ice cream at the Baskin Robbins near the movie theater. I loved living in the country. The cars, buses, and D trains of Richmond Avenue had been replaced by bikes, chirping birds, and barking dogs.

Our new school was just a few blocks away from our house, but our bus had to pick up so many other kids after us that it took a half hour to get there. Ronnie and I wanted to walk or ride our bikes instead.

"Absolutely not, Jake! You're both taking the school bus."

"But Mom! Nicky, Andy, and Simon walk."

"I don't care. I don't want you walking to school anymore."

Dad interrupted. "Honey, I think it's fine if the boys want to walk or ride their bikes to school here. This isn't Richmond Avenue."

He was right. Yonkers may have been only a short distance from the Bronx, but our street was far from Richmond Avenue. For a while anyway.

It was August 1971 when they moved in around the corner from our house. We heard they came from the city. They bought a beige house with a basketball hoop in the backyard, next door to our friend Everett. We rode our bikes to Everett's house and watched them carrying small boxes into their house as movers unloaded furniture from the truck, a big leather sofa and an enormous color TV set in a wood cabinet that looked just like ours at home.

Everett's dad appeared on his driveway wearing a sport coat and tie. Mr. Moss was an English professor at the local college. He worked from home a few afternoons each week, and whenever he saw us, he'd ask about school or our grades or our favorite subjects.

"Hi, Mr. Moss," we all said with smiles.

"Hi, boys. A little baseball today?"

"Yes, we're going to PS 26 to hit grounders," Nicky said.

"I wish I could join you. You boys excited to get back to school?"

Under duress, we nodded and mumbled an unenthusiastic yes all at once.

Mr. Moss laughed, "Alright, that was an unfair question. Go play ball and enjoy the rest of the summer." He saw his new neighbors moving in and called to Everett, "I'm going over to introduce myself. I hear they have a boy about your age."

As we rode away, Nicky said, "I'd hate it if my dad were a teacher. Is he always on your back about homework?"

"Yeah," Everett said. "We go to the library every week together. He says watching too much TV shrinks your brain."

"There is no way my dad would be going over to talk to them," Simon said.

"When my mom heard they'd bought that house, she said she didn't understand why anyone would want to move into a neighborhood where you're the only one of your kind," Nicky said. He tilted his head to the side and raised his shoulders and eyebrows. "How about your parents, Andy?"

"They said we should mind our own business and stay away from them."

"My mom and dad whisper when they talk about them. They said the neighborhood's going to hell," Simon said.

"That's funny," I said. "This morning my dad was talking about them, and he lowered his voice too. But I still heard him say they should all stay in the city where they belong."

Everett shook his head. "My dad doesn't say any of that. He said he was sure they'd be good neighbors and that they'd mow their grass and care for their new home just like everyone else in the neighborhood. He said he was going to invite them over for cocktails."

"Well, my mom and dad *definitely* aren't having cocktails with them," I said.

On the way to the ball field the others were talking and laughing. I just stared at the pavement, pedaling silently as I recalled that June day a year ago on Richmond Avenue.

* * *

Mom was trying to get the four of us off to school on time.

"Theo, J.J., your brothers are waiting. Let's go. You're gonna be late."

"We're coming."

Mom checked everyone's lunches, looked at Theo and J.J. and said, "Hold their hands when you cross the street and stay together."

They'd heard it a thousand times before. "Yes, Mom, we will."

"Have a good day at school. I'll see you at dinner."

My brothers and I piled into the elevator, glided down four floors to the lobby, and walked out of our apartment building. We squeezed through the hole in the chain-link fence and took the shortcut through a weed-filled vacant lot and passed the tenements on Brucker Street before coming out on Richmond Avenue, one block from our bus stop. Theo and J.J. held our hands as we crossed the busy street, then they let us go as we walked to the No. 8 bus, which would take us to St. Mary's Elementary School where Theo and J.J. would drop us off with the nuns before walking another block to St. Mary's High School.

We could see Theo and J.J. walking on the sidewalk ahead of us when a boy about my age and height appeared beside me. He smiled at me. I smiled back.

Showing me a blue bus ticket, the boy asked, "Do you know if my ticket is the right color for June?"

Ronnie and I shrugged. I said, "I don't know."

"Do you have a ticket?" he asked. "Can I see if yours is the same color as mine?"

I reached into my pocket for the vinyl wallet that held my monthly bus ticket and two single dollar bills Mom had given me for emergencies. I looked at the yellow ticket with the word *June* on it, but before I could say anything, the boy grabbed the wallet, shoved me to the ground, and ran off down the street.

I screamed, "Hey, he took it! He took my ticket!"

Theo and J.J. turned and rushed back to us to see what had happened. I pointed at the running boy.

"He stole my bus ticket and my money," I said.

J.J. stayed with us, and Theo took off after him. The boy crossed the street dodging traffic as the D train's roar silenced my cries. Theo was gaining on him, and as they passed a graffiti covered brick wall, the boy took a hard right turn and ran into an apartment building and down a long, dark hallway. At the end of the hallway, a door opened, and the boy ran inside. The heavy door slammed shut. Theo heard the deadbolt lock into place. He pounded on the door, but it was hopeless. The boy, my money, and my ticket were gone.

At home that night, Dad sounded like the D train. "What the hell happened?"

"We were on Richmond," Theo said, "walking to the bus stop, when we heard Jake yelling that someone took his bus ticket."

"Where were you and J.J. when his ticket was stolen?" Dad asked.

"We were with them . . ."

"If you were *with* them, how did they rob him?"

"We were a few feet in front of them, but . . ."

"Didn't your mother tell you to stay together walking to the bus stop?"

"Yes."

"So, why weren't you?"

"Dad, we were almost at the bus stop, and we were just a little bit ahead of them. It happened so fast. There were so many people on the street, we didn't think it was a . . ."

"Goddamn you two!" Veins bulged from Dad's neck. "Your mother told you to watch your brothers. You know the damn neighborhood is full of them, thieves looking to rob and steal. Both of you are gonna pay for a new bus ticket. And when you're with your brothers on Richmond, I want you *holding their hands*, you hear me?"

"Yes, Dad."

"Go do your homework."

Mom was at the table rubbing her temples.

"Eleven years old. Robbed on the street. What if that boy had hit Jake? What if he pulled a knife or a gun?"

"That's it, we're done with this goddamn city. I'm calling the broker back. We're putting a bid on that three-bedroom colonial. I'm not waiting for the foreman job."

* * *

A few days after they had moved into our neighborhood, I heard Mom and Dad whispering again in the living room. It felt like a storm had moved into our quiet neighborhood. But this storm's furious rain and violent winds weren't passing through—they were settling in. My fear and embarrassment about the robbery and my desire for Dad's approval motivated me to do the work of a spy. I began riding past the beige house searching for evidence to validate the threat to our suburban paradise. But, despite the robbery and the upheaval it caused, despite the angry voices around me, the only clues I found at the beige house were a mom pulling weeds in the front yard, a dad cleaning gutters and trimming hedges, and a boy about my age teaching his younger sister to play basketball in the backyard.

That weekend, summer was winding down, and it was hot and humid. I was laying in my hammock in the shade letting my fingertips graze the grass as I swayed. I closed my eyes, but I didn't fall asleep. I thought about the day the family had moved in with their sofa and TV that looked like ours. I remembered Everett telling us how his father was sure they'd be good neighbors. They were going to have cocktails together! I saw them pulling weeds and trimming hedges, just like Dad and I did. I opened my eyes as a fluffy cotton-like cloud eclipsed the sun and I felt a strange chill on my bare arms. That was when I began to question all the anger around me and who, exactly, had brought this bitter storm on.

A week later with the first day of school approaching, Simon and I were riding our bikes late in the afternoon when we heard a shout.

"Jake! Simon! Where are you going?"

"Is that Everett?" I asked.

We stopped our bikes in front of Everett's house as a scornful wind rustled the trees.

"Where is he?" Simon asked.

"There," I said.

We could see Everett in his new neighbor's backyard as he yelled to us again, "Jake! Simon! C'mon, you wanna play?"

Simon looked at me and said, "Nah, I don't think so. It looks like it's gonna rain anyway."

"Oh c'mon," I said. "Everett's there. If it starts raining, we'll leave."

"Really? You wanna go over there?"

"Yeah, I do."

We parked our bikes in Everett's driveway and walked through a thick wall of shrubs that separated Everett's house from the new neighbor's. The branches scratched our bare legs and arms, but we pushed through. On the other side was a manicured patch of grass and neatly tended flower beds that led to a small patio with uneven red bricks. High above the patio at the far end was a redwood deck and anchored to its side was a basketball hoop. Everett and his new neighbor were standing underneath it.

"Hey guys, this is Marlon. He's in our grade. These are my friends from around the corner, Simon and Jake."

We all said hi. Marlon was thin with wiry arms and about the same height as me.

"You wanna play a game?" Marlon asked.

"No, it's okay," I said. "You guys can finish."

"We were just shooting around," Marlon said. "We can play two-on-two, you and Simon against me and Everett."

We both shrugged and I said, "Okay."

Marlon offered me the ball. "Jake, you shoot to see who gets the ball first."

I stood at the chalked foul line, bounced it a few times and just as I shot, a gust of wind pushed the ball way to the left and it fell to the ground missing the rim and backboard. As it bounced away, Marlon ran to retrieve it.

Embarrassed, I said, "Okay, you take it out first."

Marlon handed me the ball and said, "No, the wind got it; take another shot."

Marlon smiled at me. I smiled back.

The wind calmed, and it didn't rain. We played ball together on the uneven red bricks as the fading light turned the four of us into silhouettes, all of us the same color.

CYPRESS

MY first therapist worked for St. Mark's Church on Edward Street in Buffalo, New York. I was fifteen and lived in the church's boarding school; Dr. Spiro looked about sixty. He told me that after what I'd been through, I probably should continue therapy for the foreseeable future. Two years later, after one of our sessions, he had a stroke and dropped dead. They found him behind his desk with his tape recorder still running.

His replacement, Dr. Senn, was much younger, and at our first session I asked him, "Why do the people around me keep dying?" He didn't answer that question or any of the others I'd asked him. Instead, he'd ask me what *I* thought, how *I* felt.

At one session, after some time with Dr. Senn, he asked me, "Do you ever feel that any of what happened was your fault?"

"At first, I did, right after the shock of it. But I don't feel that way now. I still think about it sometimes though. It sort of pops into my head pretty randomly. I'm sure I have some issues that—"

"Conflicts, Jon. You're conflicted about what happened with your family."

"Okay, conflicts that a doctor like you would see. But those things happened, and I can't change that. I'm dealing with my . . . conflicts in my own way, and I think I'm doing okay. I really just want to move on with my life. There are lots of things I want to do."

There were many things I never told Dr. Senn. I wrote them all down instead; it was easier to write them than talk about them. After that meeting, I realized I didn't need a therapist.

On my eighteenth birthday I signed the papers to release the now sizable trust fund left by my parents. Three months later I pulled two large empty duffel bags and a cardboard box with six years' worth of my stuff from the closet. My austere clothes fit into the two bags with room to spare, but there wasn't nearly enough emotional space in those bags for my personal possessions: the Bible given to me by Kate for my confirmation, my school report cards, the five first-day-of-school photos taken on our front doorstep and my yellow toy tractor with the moving scoop loader. Only one item insisted on coming with me: a faded Polaroid of Kate and me in front of St. Mark's church. I slipped the photo inside my diary and placed it in my bag.

At St. Mark's, I said goodbye to the few friends I'd managed to make over the years, the wonderful teachers at the boarding school and to Dr. Senn, who told me to call him if I ever wanted to talk. Tears filled my eyes as I hugged Father Collins, thanking him for all he had done for me. When I looked up at him, there were tears in his eyes too.

"God bless you, Jon. Good luck at school. Please, keep in touch."

I checked my ticket, tucked my letter of admission into my backpack, and headed to the airport for the flight back to my hometown.

After six years in dreary Buffalo, the streets of Manhattan were like a Jackson Pollock drip painting. I splurged on a hotel in Midtown for the few days before the dorms opened, and I headed to Baruch College at Lexington Avenue and 25th Street to meet with my advisor, Mr. Cardiff. Before we toured the dorms and met the professors in the literature and creative writing programs, we stopped in his office for coffee and a chat.

"Tell me, what are your hopes for your time here at Baruch?"

"Well, I want to write a novel. I guess that's no surprise, but I want it to be different."

"I think most fiction writers want to be unique, don't you?"

"Yes, but . . . well, what I mean is that ever since I was a kid I've never said much. I just sort of followed directions and went along with the crowd, you know; I didn't want to make waves. But when I write, it's like all the doors around me are swung wide open and there's no one telling me what to do or think or feel. I can write things in my stories that I could never say to someone in person."

"I understand, Jon. You're not the first person to say that to me. Writing is a wonderful outlet. And college is an experience that changes people and pushes them to grow. I look forward to hearing your voice change and grow on the page."

In my four years at Baruch and in the years after, some things did change for me. Some didn't.

* * *

If it had been up to me to say hello, we'd never have met. It was a New Year's Day Bowl Game party in the East Village, and she walked right up to me and started talking.

"Hi, I'm Lucinda. You're Jon, right?"

Spilling only a few drops of my beer, I said, "Yes, hi, do I know you?"

"We have mutual friends who know the host—Cheryl and Jeff from your building. Cheryl knows I'm a world-class party crasher, and she knew you were coming, so she suggested that I say hello. You're the writer who waits tables at O'Connor's on 10th Street?"

"Yes, that's me. I guess Cheryl gave you a description: tall, dark hair."

"Uh huh," she said, with a quick raise of her eyebrows and a sly grin.

"There are a few other guys here with dark hair. How many tries did it take to find me?"

"Actually, you were my first try. Cheryl said you're the quiet type and you'd probably be standing near the bar watching the game."

Lucinda and I were both twenty-five years old and five foot eleven. She had athletic arms that she enjoyed showing off, shoulder-length blond hair, and high, pink cheekbones that contrasted her fair skin. She grinned at the too-busy bartender and said to him, "You don't mind if I help myself." It wasn't a question. Before he could say a word, she had poured two margaritas from his pitcher, and we moved to a quieter corner.

"Cheryl said you were born in New York, but you moved to Buffalo before coming back for school?"

"Yeah, I moved there when I was twelve."

"Parents get jobs there?"

"No, they died in a car accident, so I went to live with a cousin."

"How awful. You were so young." Her words and expression took on a seriousness that seemed oddly devoid of empathy. "Do you have any siblings?"

"No, just me." I changed the subject, "So, tell me about you. Where are you from?"

Her smile reappeared instantly, "New York, born and raised. I have a tiny apartment in Union Square. After NYU I got recruited by a big ad agency downtown, Publicom. I just got promoted to work with our top account executive. I work with some big clients, Fortune 500 types. Lots of pressure, but I like it."

"Writing a novel alone in my bedroom gives me all the pressure I can handle."

For the next hour, we drank margaritas and talked about work, music, clubs, food. Mostly, it was Lucinda talking. I was content watching her decisive hands move in unison with her bright eyes and fluid lips, all coordinated to project a vigorous and charming energy.

"Cheryl's read a few of your short stories. She said you're very talented. Said you're going to be famous someday. Have you published anything?"

"A few pieces in literary journals."

She gulped the last of her margarita, "Well, maybe we should get together sometime so you can . . . show me some of your work."

With that, she reached into her bag and handed me a Post-it note and a small pen, which I snatched from her hand with surprising speed before fumbling it to the floor.

We exchanged numbers, and she asked, "How about we have a shot and get outta here? They have my favorite whiskey."

"What's that?"

"Fireball."

By the time we grabbed our coats, she already had the Uber on her phone. The destination was Union Square.

For the first few months, our relationship was a blast. We had some disagreements that new couples have, and Lucinda was more vocal about them than I was, but mostly, we enjoyed our time together. Then, in April, she stumbled into a pair of tickets to a weekend jazz festival in Virginia.

"Lucinda, I can't go. I promised Jerry I'd read his manuscript this weekend."

"Can't you read it Monday?"

"His deadline is Monday; I've got to do it this weekend."

"There are four other people in your writing group. Couldn't he ask someone else to read it? Tell him we unexpectedly got these great tickets for *this* weekend. He'll understand.

"I'm the only one in town, and I made a commitment. I can't back out at the last minute."

"Make something up, some emergency. He'll understand."

"I can't lie to him. I wouldn't be able to look at him at our meetings."

"So, you're willing to screw up an awesome weekend because you're afraid to disappoint some guy you've known for six months."

"I'm not afraid, it's—"

"Jon, you constantly do this. You let people walk all over you. Last weekend at Zabar's, you didn't say a word to the jerk who cut the line; I had to shame him. And that sneaky move by your landlord changing the sublet rights in your lease—you were just going to accept it. I'm the one who had to call him. You need to stand up for yourself. You're too fragile, always worried about what people will think. You know, being a little selfish every now and then doesn't make you a bad person."

We went to the festival, but I brought the manuscript and read it between shows. The next day she ended our relationship. I wasn't worth the investment, even if I might someday become a successful writer.

At home that night, I uncorked a bottle of Basil Hayden bourbon and poured a heavy shot over ice, followed by two more. Normally, three encounters with Mr. Hayden would invite slurring, wobbling, and an early bedtime, but that night, I received an unexpected visit from the shadowy face of Dr. Senn, now with a gray beard, floating above my couch.

His voice had a strange echo, *"Jon, why do you think you were attracted to Lucinda?"*

"Oh, I know why, and if I had told you everything I was feeling back in Buffalo, you'd know why too."

"Tell me now. I'd like to hear what you think it is."

"Well, it's complicated. All the women I've known since college have been the same: assertive and fearless. Chloe risked everything she had to start her own company at eighteen. Kitt was charming, but she ran over people to get ahead. And Lucinda had incredible positive energy; she just couldn't live with the knowledge that someone had taken advantage of her. It sounds weird—I was attracted to them, but I disliked who they were."

"Hmm, so your attraction was just physical?"

"No, I mean, yes, I was physically attracted to all of them, but that wasn't the only reason. I told you it's complicated. Lucinda said I wasn't selfish enough, but I dated all of them because they had something I wanted."

"What was that?"

"All the things that made them people I disliked. How's that for a conflict, Doc? I wanted to be assertive and fearless like they were. They were able to deal with life's confrontations and threats and clear a path toward their own self-interest. I wanted what they had so desperately that I was willing to pay for access to it with the currency of my own unhappiness. They were all transactional relationships that allowed me to avoid all the confrontations that were too intimidating or painful to deal with on my own. I traded away true happiness for a shield."

"*Do you think you were being duplicitous?*"

"Yes! And I have never felt right about it, but it was never malicious."

"*Then why did you put yourself through it?*"

"Because I knew the value of what they had. I saw what happens to *nice* people, *forgiving* people. I knew that egoism is sometimes better than generosity."

"*You learned that the hard way, didn't you Jon?*"

I stared at the bearded face that was now hovering inches above me as if taunting me. "Yeah, it's still inside me, that . . . conflict."

* * *

Their car had skidded off an icy road, rolled down an embankment, and struck a giant oak tree. My parents' attorney, following the terms of their will, arranged for Kate, my mother's cousin in Buffalo, to be my legal guardian. Kate was forty-six and had always wanted children. She never had any luck finding a husband, until earlier that year when she married Blaine, a twice divorced ne'er-do-well with beguiling charm, a great love of whiskey, and very little interest in raising children. Kate married him because she liked having someone to take care of but mostly because she believed in redemption and second chances. Blaine enjoyed being cared for, but mostly he married Kate because the mortgage on her house was paid off.

Kate was a kind woman. On the day I arrived, her appearance was neat and proper. She wore a modest dress and spoke with the hushed assuredness of a kindergarten teacher calming one of her charges at naptime.

"You poor child, you've had such terrible misfortune with your mama and papa, God rest their souls."

She handed me an eight inch square box wrapped in gold paper tied with a red bow.

"Open it, Jon. It's a little something to welcome you to your new home."

Inside the box was a yellow Caterpillar tractor with big black rubber wheels and a loading scoop that moved up and down.

I sheepishly said, "Thank you."

"You're welcome sweetheart. I've fixed up your very own room. Would you like to see it?"

We walked up the stairs and into my room. Kate sat on my bed, which was covered with red and blue Buffalo Bills players, took both of my hands into hers, and said, "Jon, I promise I'm going to take care of you. Don't you worry."

Soon, I learned that Sunday mornings were special to Kate. While Blaine slept off his Saturday night whiskey, Kate and I attended church, where our youthful new priest, Father Collins, framed the ancient words of Christ into sermons crafted for the twenty-first century and the impressionable teens in the parish. Throughout those services, Kate would praise God, but I could only ask Him why.

Blaine was a different sort, callous and blunt especially when Kate wasn't around. He welcomed me by saying, "Just deal with it, boy. You're lucky I agreed to take you in."

Hearing the snarl in his words and imagining his quick rage, I held back tears and offered a nod of my head. It was that way for the next few years. My words, when I found the courage to speak, were few and carefully chosen. It wasn't hard to know that his generosity in taking me in had less to do with luck and more to do with the trust fund my parents had left me.

Two years later, when he was fired from his construction job, he dealt with his disappointment by mixing his whiskey with violence. Kate took to wearing large sunglasses and long sleeves. Through devout tears and desecrating bruises, she vowed to leave him, but Blaine, knowing she was the forgiving type, summoned his own beastly powers, and with spurious apologies he'd wipe clear Kate's promises to leave him, just like so many of her tears.

"Why do you still love him? Why don't you send him away for good?"

"Darling Jon, I couldn't do that to him. He needs me, and we vowed to stay together for better or for worse. Everything will be alright; you'll see."

One afternoon I came home from school and heard blaring voices from the television. I tiptoed up the stairs. Kate and Blaine were in their bedroom. I glanced inside, and my palms began to sweat. I walked slowly through the hallway and back down to the kitchen to do what I should have done weeks before; I called the police. When they arrived, they saw the house strewn with broken promises, in the whiskey bottles, in the bruises on her face, and in the tears of a 15-year-old boy. Father Collins arrived and held me by my shoulders, and we looked, wordlessly, into each other's eyes. He pulled me close, and I began to cry. I could feel his breath shudder with emotion. He ushered me away from the house so I wouldn't have to see all the harrowing police activity. Then, wiping my tears, he promised that he'd find a place for me to stay, as if I could still believe in promises.

"I should have done something," I said. "She couldn't send him away. S-She needed me. I should have helped her."

"It's not your fault, Jon."

"I didn't know Blaine had a gun."

I looked past the priest and watched the police van drive away with the bodies.

* * *

Feeling awe for the mist of 750,000 gallons of water pouring over Niagara Falls every second is one reason to travel to Buffalo, New York. I had another good reason to visit. But not even my seven years in New York could suppress my inner turmoil about that place and all that I'd lived through there. I had left Buffalo sure that I didn't need any more therapy, but it was a bourbon-induced therapy session with myself that convinced me to make the trip.

It was 74 degrees on the Saturday afternoon in July when I arrived in Buffalo for a visit with Father Collins and a few of my old teachers. During my college years, Father Collins and I had emailed each other monthly, but as time passed, it became one or two messages a year. He was probably close to forty years old now, but he still had the look of a college student with his stylish eyeglasses and long brown hair framing his thin face. On Saturday night, the five of us piled into a church van with tickets for a Buffalo Bisons ballgame. Over lukewarm hotdogs and watery beer, they thanked me for the annual contributions I was making to the church, and each of them shared the news of the parish, the school, and the local community. It was a raucous and amusing evening seeing these old role models cutting loose like my old college buddies.

On Sunday morning I attended the ten o'clock mass at St. Mark's. I hadn't been to church since I'd left Buffalo, but I didn't have the heart to disappoint Father Collins. I sat in the front pew feigning prayer and smiling in agreement during his homily. After the service he invited me to his office and closed the door.

"Yesterday was great fun with the guys, but I thought it'd be nice for you and me to chat. I think about you often, Jon. I'd love to hear more about life in New York."

"I love it. My friends would probably say that I spend too much time on my novel, but it's what I want to do."

"Are they close, your friends? I mean, can you *talk* to them?

"Yes, and I do. They all know what happened, and they're very supportive. I'm still working out some of my . . . conflicts, but I'm fine, really."

"If you don't mind my asking, how's your social life otherwise?"

I laughed, "You mean, am I seeing anyone. I was dating a girl a few months ago, but we broke it off. It wasn't serious. I've moved on."

"Sorry to hear that. It's a big city. I'm sure you'll meet someone wonderful." He clapped his hands and rubbed them together. "Hey, how about I show you the new school building."

We walked around the block and past the old school,

which was now a day care center run by the church. In the old vacant lot on Edward St., there stood a new St. Mark's Boarding School, twice as large as the old one.

"It's all new, except for one thing. Can you find it?"

As I scanned the building, Father Collins watched me with an expectant grin on his face.

"You kept the doors," I said.

"Right. They are the originals built in 1880. We couldn't leave them out of the new building."

The grand, eight-foot tall set of arched doors were fashioned from three-inch thick cypress wood with black wrought-iron hardware. There were Biblical scenes carved in intricate relief on each of six squares. The ethereal reliefs glistened with a deep mahogany-hued varnish as if dispensing some silent message to all who regarded them.

"They're beautiful. I'm glad you kept them," I said.

"God's wisdom is there in those scenes: benevolence toward our brothers, faith, trust, generosity of spirit. All of it captured in the delicate and fragile artistry. And as fragile as the doors look, the cypress they're made from stands up to Buffalo's harshest cold and ice and wind."

I paused, transfixed by the reliefs that I hadn't appreciated as a boy passing through them every day. "What was that you said, Father?"

"What I mean is, well, delicate things can also be powerful, especially when they present good intentions."

Buffalo Niagara Airport was crowded on Sunday evening as I sat at the gate waiting to board my flight back to New York. At the next gate, a tall man wearing a fedora was preparing to board his flight. I heard the gate agent tell him that his carry-on bag was too big and that he'd have to gate-check it. He told the agent it wasn't oversized, a debate ensued, and he insisted that they measure it. I and several other passengers watched that scene and looked down at our shoes or our phones. Several minutes later, I could feel the muscles of my face evolving from an uneasy frown to a broad smile as the man in the fedora thanked the gate agent and boarded his flight sporting a satisfied smile of his own and his carry-on bag.

NOT EVEN OUR BROTHERS

He pressed his forehead against mine,
clasped me round the waist, and said that
henceforth we were married; meaning, in
his country's phrase, that we were bosom
friends; he would gladly die for me, if need
should be.

—Melville, *Moby Dick*

THE rain fell on Larry Fender's casket without passion or prejudice. Years ago, at a party, when asked what he did for a living, Larry answered, "I'm an attorney in the Manhattan DA's office." The party guest, loosened by bourbon, pursued his line of questioning further and asked whether public opinion, political pressure, or even personal prejudices ever affected his work prosecuting alleged criminals. With a half-smile and a tilt of his head, Larry answered, "The only things I carry into the courtroom are the facts and the law; everything else is left outside the door." The cold December rain fell everywhere, guided only by Nature's dispassion. It fell on the parking lot, it fell on the trees, it fell on the mourners, it fell on Larry Fender's casket, all as if a lovely homage to the man inside.

Larry Fender, James Budd, Leo Cohen, and I, Alex LaChance, met fifty-three years ago at Soaring Oak Elementary School in the Westchester suburb of Scarsdale, outside New York City. I'm convinced Nature sorts adolescent boys into groups. The four of us weren't leather-jacket-wearing greasers or stellar academics bound for Harvard or romantics who, in the pine trees behind the gymnasium, divined the pleasure of kissing girls. Rather than compete with fists, textbooks, or embarrassment in the pine trees, the four of us played ball: basketball, football, baseball, any ball. If the weather was foul, we moved to Larry's basement, where we played ping-pong or cards while listening to music on his father's stereo system. Not Mr. Fender's Haydn or Debussy or Mozart— we had our own Holy Trinity of music: drums, bass, and lead guitar. We were inseparable and managed to avoid typical childhood disagreements. When we weren't playing ball or listening to music, we rode our bikes to get ice cream, hiked to the distant side of Lake Woodcrest, or enjoyed scavenger hunts in the deep woods behind old man Dolen's property. We were a gang of four best friends, but it was James and I who shared a deeper, closer bond. I'm not sure why he chose me because there was nothing exceptional about me.

James Budd, however, was gifted. He couldn't run very fast, and his strange habit of eating peanut butter and jelly sandwiches every day for lunch earned him the nickname Skippy. But the name never stuck, and I knew why. There was a kindness in James that was unusual for a 12-year-old boy. You could hear it in his voice as he calmed a crying third grader who couldn't find his classroom on the first day of school and see it in his eyes as he missed our school bus home so he could help a kid who'd gotten hurt falling off his bike. The teachers all said that James was a "such a caring boy." I called it his gift. The only thing James wanted in return for his gift was a smile. The name didn't stick because James Budd had too big a heart to be defined by some frivolous nickname.

After graduation, we all enrolled at colleges around New York, and no one was surprised that James and I were accepted at the same school and became roommates. For us, a key purpose of college was partying, but even someone as unexceptional as me was able to grasp one of the true gifts of college: being incited by books and classmates and professors to think more deeply and to ask questions about things I thought I knew. Not just intellectual things—I also thought about friends and relationships. How, in elementary school, my friends were the kids I sat next to in class. How, in high school, I thought that such a precious thing as true friendship should be born of something less random than the serendipity of a seating chart. And, how, in college, I became sure of it, sure of some complex combination of forces at work to determine what type of people we become, how we think the world works, who we choose as friends, and more significantly, which of them goes beyond being the friend who helps us move furniture and rises to that often singular place in our lives reserved for our *fidus Achates*, a friend from whom no secret is kept and with whom no sorrow is too burdensome. At our weddings, when James and I stood for each other as best man, it surprised no one, not even our brothers.

But there were secrets that James kept, and it took many years before I learned of them. He kept them not to protect his own privacy or some *thing* he valued, but rather to protect me from the unease, that awkward touch of guilt I might feel knowing the things he'd done, with considerable inconvenience, or even cost, in service to me. And years later, when James's actions were unwittingly shared with me, I did feel that unease, and it magnified the shame I felt knowing I might not make the same magnanimous sacrifices for a friend. Stories of broken dates with his girlfriend Erica, his aborted impromptu weekend ski trip with her, his abandoned lunch with a recruiter to discuss a coveted IBM internship. I'm sure he made plausible excuses to those he disappointed. There were just other things he needed to attend to. My broken ankle that turned out to be a sprain; my twenty-page presentation left behind in our dorm room with only one way to get delivered in time for my speech at a marketing conference in New York City. And Maria's disclosure, after too much wine, of her neighbor Grace's heartbreaking ordeal. The crushing middle-of-the-night abandonment by her husband leaving her and their two young sons to make sense of it all through their tears. Her wealthy brother in California refusing to help even though he had the means. James paying the daycare costs for the boys while Grace went back to school for a teaching certificate. Those things were just money out of James' pocket. It was what he did with his time that made me question the size of my own heart. There were visits to the library with the boys, hot dogs at Yankee games. He coached their little league team. He cheered when the boys mastered their two-wheelers and gave solace when they skinned their knees. He was the most patient of driving instructors. All this, without ever neglecting his own family. Each was a choice, a choice he made freely. The truth was, there was never really a choice at all. It was a gift.

The recitation of Kaddish stopped the rain. The shock of Larry's death added considerable weight to the shovelful of wet dirt I placed into his grave. I approached Larry's widow Angela and held her limp body. Our silent embrace amid choked tears connected us in a way that words could not, and I was startled with a precious and consoling insight that the act of healing could be so simple. All of us, James and Maria, Leo and Lori, Abby and I, dried our eyes and walked to our cars for the short drive to the restaurant where lunch had been arranged.

The restaurant was a respite from the duplicitous scent of flowers—celebration at weddings, sorrow at funerals. All of us ate together, except James. I saw him sitting in a corner with Larry's daughters, Jaden and Zoe, college girls with mascara smudges on their cheeks, doing his best to reset the orbit of their world. After lunch, as we said our goodbyes, everyone hugged Angela. These weren't normal good-bye hugs; these lasted just a second longer. How was it possible that a single extra second of time could carry so much meaning? I looked at Abby to see if she was ready to go, but she and Maria had begun a conversation with Angela and the look on her face told me she couldn't leave. They decided they would go back to Angela's and stay with her for a while, so James and I drove into town for a much-needed drink.

Poe's Tavern had been Larry's favorite place for a Saturday afternoon beer. He had a preferred table against the wall by the fireplace where he'd tell us stories about the wild things jurors had said during voir dire, or his recurrent dream of running for public office, or the pro bono work he'd done for a local shelter for abused women. Poe's was founded in 1894 by a man who wrote stories and poems as a hobby. It was now owned by his great-granddaughter, an older woman with a vigor in her step, a fondness for old scotch, and a vocabulary fit for a barroom. She wasn't a writer; she was a librarian by trade. Some years ago, she added several bookshelves to the tavern walls and filled them with classic novels and books of poetry for patrons who, liberated by the spirits, might be compelled to read a few lines of Homer or Shakespeare or Melville, either quietly to themselves or raucously to their gathered friends. Poe's was a charismatic and convivial place to spend an afternoon with a glass and a companion, living or dead.

The tavern's heavy wooden door, sturdy oak floor-boards, hewn wood beams, and stone fireplace had remained unchanged since its opening. The most curious feature of Poe's, however, was its century-old woodwork. The tavern's walls were fashioned and trimmed with fine grain persimmon wood in an ebony color, which, depending on the angle of sunlight, changed in tone and mood. The walls' richness and changeability were seductive, almost sentient. The bartenders were fond of recounting the local myth that these protean walls were in fact a historical ledger of sorts, whose mood and color were imbued in the grain not by some exotic pigment but rather by having stood as a silent and receptive audience to one hundred years of daring tales, solemn confessions, and whispered dreams.

Poe's thirty-foot-long bar had been worn smooth by thousands of hands over the decades. Above it, the founder had hung an antique stained-glass triptych, whose presence was so magisterial it couldn't be ignored. In a medley of opulent colors, it depicted the three Greek divinities Clotho, Lachesis, and Atropos, in bold stances as if defending the massive bar from worldly obtruders, their names etched in delicate ribbons of deep crimson glass.

James and I took a table near the fireplace. We warmed our hands with the fire and our stomachs with a 12-year-old scotch.

"Maria said something strange to me this morning while we were getting dressed," James said.

"What was it?"

"She asked me how long I expected to live."

"Did she have a knife in her hand when she asked?"

"No, Alex, Maria's more of shotgun girl—you know, keep her manicure neat."

"Why would that question surprise you, under the circumstances?"

"I suppose, but asking me how long I expect to live? The word *expect* seemed strange. It feels different than asking, how long do you *think* you'll live. *Think* gives it a more casual tone, like a passing comment, you know, shooting the breeze. Using *expect* makes it sound like a serious question, one I should give some serious thought to before answering. Don't you think?"

"You're an engineer, James. I think you think too much about everything. Whether she said *think* or *expect*, either way I don't think it's a strange question on a day like this. What did you say?"

"I told her that I don't think about dying. I get up every day and live my life, and I expect to wake up again tomorrow. But who knows? It's fate. Larry was still taking judo classes; he had normal blood pressure, good cholesterol, and taking out the trash ends up killing him. His time was up. Some things are just out of our control. We should just enjoy life every day," James said.

We looked at each other, and I said, "Alright, that's enough depression for one day. Let's talk about something fun. How about retirement? I figure we both have a good thirty years left. For two guys who hate their jobs as much as we do, is there anything as exciting as thinking about thirty years of retirement?"

"Yeah, to not feel nauseous on Sunday nights thinking about Monday morning. A couple more years, if I can stand it, and I'll be ready to pack it in. Maria loves her job, so she'll probably keep working."

"Abby and I need another two or three years. Neither of us wants to do anything fancy though—no beach house or around the world cruise. Abby wants to audit some college classes, do some traveling, and hopefully at some point there'll be grandkids. And I know exactly what I want to do with my free time."

"I think I can guess, but go ahead, let's hear it."

"I'm going to do the two things I've always loved but never had time for: woodworking and writing. I'm going to convert part of the garage so I can work on small wood projects like my dad used to do. And I'm finally going to write a book."

"Well, you've been talking about that since college, so it's about time."

"Once I'm done working, I'll have the time to actually do it. And now I know what I want to write: something of substance that will tell my grandchildren, knock wood, something about me to keep a bit of myself alive for them after I'm gone."

"That sounds like a great idea. A memoir," James said. "I hope we all have lots of grandkids."

I followed James's eyes as he spoke to the fireplace surrounded by the ancient stone and sable colored walls. "Damn it, Larry. Weddings and grandkids and travel, that's all you ever talked about."

We held up our glasses and drank to Larry.

"He's probably listening and waiting for us to order another scotch and finish our retirement conversation," James said.

"Well, he'd agreed that after forty years of jobs that made us ill, we should finally do what *we* want to do. No boss, no clock, no pressure. I plan on spending the rest of my life, however long it is, doing the things I love. We know Larry would have traveled the world. How about you? What are the two or three things you want to spend your time doing?"

I waited for James to speak, but he had a confused smile on his face as though he'd never given any thought to the question of what things made him happy. He stared, first at me, then again at the 100-year-old woodwork by the fireplace, which in the afternoon light had changed to an inky violet. He bit his lower lip, struggling to answer. How unfair it was that the gift of an enormous heart was no guarantee that you could recognize your own happiness.

One of our four had died a sudden and insolent death, and as we sat beside the attentive wall, now charcoal gray, I was speaking of a propitious light on my horizon, but the friend I loved most in the world, the friend who loved the most, could not find the breath to whisper his dream.

UNCLE JOHN

HE greeted me with a bright smile, "Your name please?"

"Julian Serra."

I handed him my driver's license and the first of three monogrammed Briggs & Riley suitcases. He checked my bags while I checked my phone.

"You're all set, Mr. Serra. Flight 274 to JFK is on time. That's gate 51 boarding at ten thirty. One way, first class, seat 1B." With another bright smile he asked, "So, are you moving to New York?"

To a Midwesterner, that question would be the start of a neighborly conversation between two strangers brought together by happenstance. Midwestern Julian would have offered a convivial backstory and some superfluous banter, all according to the courteous rules that insist on friendly dialogue in such encounters. But I'm not a Midwesterner. I'm not even a chill coastal Californian. I'm a devout Northeasterner, a native New Yorker with no interest in mock pleasantries when there's nothing to be gained or anything of value to be learned. So what? I was moving to New York. Would he want to know why I was traveling alone, too? "Look, I really don't have time for a conversation. Can I have my baggage stubs?"

"I'm sorry, sir. We don't see too many one-way passengers."

"You've got a line of customers behind me who would probably be pretty pissed off if we started a conversation."

"Just trying to be cordial with you, sir."

"Fine, whatever."

"That's gate 51. Have a good flight."

I turned to leave and paused. *Why do I do this?* I turned back. "Look, it's nothing personal; I'm a little tired. I need to get to the lounge and close my eyes for a while. Thanks; have a nice day."

"You as well, sir."

Nine years in sunny, laid back LA hadn't thawed the ice of my previous eighteen growing up in New York, a city that, at least in my Bronx neighborhood, bred a thick skin, quick wit, fast moves, cynicism toward the motives of outsiders, and a general impatience and distaste for inefficient people and outcomes that didn't meet my expectations. There was at least one place in LA that welcomed, even celebrated, my New Yorkness: the equity trading desk at Klein Brothers. There, my overbearing style allowed me to reap absurdly large financial rewards.

Arden Strom used a different toolkit to earn her success when she arrived at the M&A department at Klein Brothers. Her gears turned less abrasively than mine. She was a profitable and prolific dealmaker in the company, and she managed to do it with a mix of intellect, business savvy, and irresistible geniality, making all parties at the negotiating table feel as though they had come away with the better deal.

Arden had only heard about the cynical New Yorker on the trading desk. When our paths finally crossed at an after-work happy hour, it was hard to misread the physical attraction between us. It was instantaneous and intense, like the attraction of opposite poles on two magnets. "Are you always this funny?" she asked. I was both flummoxed and enchanted by the sincerity and complete lack of sarcasm in her question. She was openly delighted by my inability to fire off some snarky East Coast response. Finally, I managed to stammer, "Really? Uh, thank you." Weeks later, she would be equally delighted by my offer to give her visiting brother and sister a tour of LA and to cook dinner for us at her apartment. After that dinner, it was to my delight and surprise when I overheard Arden tell her sister, "He's like an egg—hard on the outside, soft on the inside."

We were the poster couple for opposites attracting, in our styles both at work and at home. I, the brusque New York bachelor, was determined to decorate my apartment with a California coastal vibe. It was an epic mess of palm leaves, surf gear, and wicker, all dominated by a 60-inch flat screen television on the wall. When Arden saw the chaos I'd created, she cheerfully commented, "Wow, it's so . . . California."

"It didn't come out like I thought it would."

"Well, it's a bachelor pad. It's supposed to look . . . comfortable. I think it's great."

Her apartment was out of a magazine, a sleek contemporary affair. Even the strange touch of pillows in zesty, clashing colors crocheted by her Aunt Lena seemed to work when guided by her relaxed hand.

"I know they look goofy," she said, "but they remind me of home. And they do warm the place up, don't you think?"

The inarguable grace of her Minnesotaness was a cure to my insolent New Yorkness. She wasn't rude to amiable airline ticket agents. She'd have said, "He was just being friendly." And I would have looked at her face, a bright water-color with curves of dense blond hair, blush cheeks, and large round eyeglasses that accentuated her wide-set blue eyes, and all I could have said was, yes, Arden.

Arden seemed pleased with her ability to cast this benev-olence over me. I could sense her gratification that she could soften the rough edges of the guy with the brash reputation who made her laugh so easily. Her kind affability toward everyone, so foreign to my sensibilities, incited me to ear-nest pledges of self-transformation from cynic to optimist. But her powers proved temporary. Like a motor running out of gas, my very nature would unconsciously abandon my pledges. Should a restaurant run out of the special entrée after our waiter took my order, the maître d' was berated. If our deluxe hotel room was replaced by a slightly less deluxe yet still wonderful room, arrogant hell was raised with the manager. When an apologetic Uber driver misunderstood the directions and steered us into a hopelessly choked avenue, cruel words would be mumbled about foreigners needing to learn English. And always, there was Arden, who, unwilling to participate in my pompous and petty callousness, could only look away.

A gruff temperament is one thing, but I had another peculiarity that perplexed not only Arden but myself as well, although she never pressed me about it. I don't think I could have explained why whenever I saw the possibility of an impromptu encounter with an acquaintance or neighbor, on a street, or in a grocery store, I made an abrupt effort to avoid the meeting. I assumed that for the rest of the human population, these chance meetings were happy occasions for effortless, congenial conversation. For me, they were an agonizing chore of choosing an acceptable topic, editing my words to evoke appealing charm rather than clumsy excess, lip-biting speculation as to whether this person even *wants* to talk to me. My groundless overthink would culminate in a single anxious thought: *What will they think of me?* How could an admittedly overbearing New Yorker explain to Arden, or anyone, these neurotic feelings of inferiority and social discomfort that would cause me to cross the street to avoid an interaction, not with some stranger who held no influence in my life but with my own next-door neighbor?

We lasted about six months. It ended without a fight, just a quiet conversation and mutual feelings of disappointment. She told me that she didn't understand why I needed everything to be "just so," that she was unhappy and saddened by my arrogant moments with waiters and cab drivers, by my impatience and inflexibility, but she never suspected a corruption in me, only a vulnerability. She said there was a kindness buried in me, waiting to be excavated. I insisted that I wasn't good for her, that I was a corrosive, dulling a shiny gem stroke by stroke, that it was in my nature, that I was the cause of her unhappiness.

I didn't know how to fix it, and I didn't want to break it any further, so I left her. I left with an insuppressible feeling that I could have said more, should have done more. I left with a lone seat on flight 274. As the flight attendant closed the door, my seat mate for the next five hours eased into

seat 1A, smiled at me, and remarked that my drink looked
like a good idea. I sensed a friendly question coming, *"Is it
Champagne or a sparkling wine from Napa?"* I looked him in
the eye, and before he could say another word, I put on my
noise cancelling headphones and closed my eyes.

The New York office of Klein Brothers was in lower
Manhattan, a twenty-minute walk from my new apartment
in SoHo. When Arden and I had visited New York, we'd
stayed in SoHo. She raved about its urban, artistic vibe saying this was where she'd live if she ever moved to New York.
Her smooth gears were able to shift enthusiastically from
LA's sunny groove to New York's brazen urgency.

I bought a small, neglected loft on Broome Street for
$2.8 million. It was a solid investment with an ocean of nat-
ural light crashing through its enormous windows. I hired a
decorator. She installed a stainless steel Poggenpohl kitchen,
smooth concrete floors, exposed industrial duct work hung
from fourteen-foot matte black ceilings, and a low-slung, red
Roche Bobois leather sectional. On my first day there, I took
a nap on that red leather with my head resting on a prepos-
terous sixteen-inch green-and-orange crocheted pillow.

During my time in LA, my brother Burton had moved
from New York to Austin, but Uncle Vic and Aunt Teddi
were in their eighties and still living on Staten Island. Teddi
called me shortly after I arrived, thrilled I had moved back to
New York, but the real purpose of her call was to ask a favor.

"You remember Uncle John . . . Caracelli."

"Of course, I remember Uncle John." They had always

been *Uncle* John and *Aunt* Emma even though we weren't related.

"Well, he had a fall on the street outside his apartment. He got banged up and hurt his knee. He was in the hospital for a day being checked for a concussion, but he's okay, and he's back home. Anyway, he could use some help while his knee heals."

"What about his son? Can he help him?"

"George still lives in Hong Kong."

"Does he have neighbors who could help?"

"Oh, the two other jerks in his building never say a word to him. Uncle Vic and I don't drive in the city anymore, and we can't manage the ferry and subway. Anyway, Burton called me yesterday and told me you had moved back to New York, and I thought, what a blessing. Julian, do you think you could help? He still lives uptown near the park. Just one or two visits a week for a couple of weeks is all, to pick up groceries and medication. He really needs the help, and he'd love to see you again."

This was definitely not in my plan, but what could I say. He was like family. I just hoped he didn't have dementia or that sour old-person smell. I'd drop off his groceries, hang out for twenty minutes, and leave.

"Sure, I'll do it Aunt Teddi. Give me his number and I'll call him."

* * *

In January 1966, the body of Father Philip Caracelli arrived in New York. His injuries had been so severe that the casket was closed. My parents were at his funeral at Our Lady of Mount Carmel Church on a windy, frigid morning. Dad remembered every moment. Uncle John gave the eulogy for his older and only brother. He squeezed the edges of the oak pulpit, inhaled deeply, and shared the letter from the Army describing how Philip was giving last rites to a dying soldier on the edge of a rain-soaked jungle when a mortar struck. Then, Uncle John looked at the dark crowd and, with a quivering voice, said, "My mother told me that the first word I spoke as a child was not Dada or yes, it was Phip." He paused and regripped the pulpit. "On the day he left for Vietnam, Philip told me that he volunteered so that he could offer a living representation of Christ to our soldiers. My big brother has inspired me since my first words, he still inspires me, but never more so than on that day." Dad told me it was the only time he ever saw Uncle John lose control of himself.

After the funeral, everyone said they saw the change in Uncle John. It was a sadness of course, but also an acceptance, and a new intention, a keen awareness of not only of life's fragility but of all the beauty it had to offer while we are here.

John and Emma Caracelli had been dear friends of my mother's family in the Bronx since their childhood in the 1940s. Aunt Emma died six years ago, and Uncle John was still living in the second floor apartment they bought in 1970 on 84th Street and Columbus Avenue. When I was a young boy, they would visit us in the Bronx around the holidays. The two were unlike the rest of my family. Aunt Emma had a more feminine quality than my mom and aunts. She was soft-spoken with thin gray hair pulled back tightly, and she walked as if on eggshells. She never used foul language like

Aunt Constance, and instead of drinking beer like Mom and Aunt Teddi, she sipped cordials, but never in a pretentious way. Uncle Vic and Uncle Sonny were products of their tough Bronx neighborhood and their divorces. They owned a printing shop together, which supported their alimony payments and the weekly bets they laid down on horses, numbers, and football games. Sundays were often reserved for visits to our house where they'd drink Rheingold beer, smoke Chesterfields, and watch the Giants or Yankees on television.

Uncle John, dressed in a suit and tie, was disinterested in sports. He would entertain my father, who didn't live the raucous life of his brothers, with conversation. They would reminisce with sweet stories of old friends from the neighborhood or distant relatives still in Italy.

Uncle John was in his sixties then and a tailor by trade. He was an average-looking man, portly, with thinning gray hair and large silver-rimmed eyeglasses that hung on large ears. His rounded forehead was sprinkled with liver spots, and his jowls hung in soft layers that shook when he laughed, which was often. He never attended college, but through his conversation, his lyrical voice with its precise diction, his duet of demonstrative hand movements and thoughtful cadence of speech, I sensed that he was saying important things, things of value, things worth remembering, things my young ears could only presume to be wisdom.

Uncle John and Aunt Emma seemed as though they were from some other world located on a higher ground, a place where people visited museums, listened to classical music and read voraciously. My father had no experience of the higher place they inhabited. But by his eagerness to ignore his beloved Yankees on TV and his enthusiasm in listening to Uncle John, it was clear that he had tremendous admiration for his knowledge and eloquence, traits that, in another life, my father might delight in possessing himself. Most curious to both my father and me was Uncle John's custom of writing letters and poetry, the latter of which he would share with us during Sunday dessert and coffee. The words were written in the elegant cursive of a schoolteacher, not only in English, but often in Italian. Sadly, a true and full appreciation of this unique man was hobbled by my insular adolescence.

* * *

I had originally planned to visit old friends in Brooklyn on Saturday, but after I called my uncle, I was committed. As I sipped coffee looking down on a morning dogwalker on Broome Street, I prepared some fiction that would get me out of Uncle John's apartment as quickly as possible. Then, something I hadn't thought of raised a concern about my involvement, however temporarily, in the care of my uncle. Would this make me the official caretaker of an 83-year-old man? My cynicism told me that I was making a big mistake.

I rode the C train uptown to 86th Street. In the warm light of a September afternoon, I made my way along the crowded sidewalk to Fairway Grocery where I picked up the few items on Uncle John's grocery list. As I approached the steps of his quintessential New York brownstone, I wondered what he had paid for this apartment in 1970 and what it was worth today. I pressed the buzzer, and a second later he buzzed me in. The elevator took me to the second floor where his apartment door swung open. Uncle John's knee injury hadn't affected his mood.

"Julian my boy, so good to see you. Come in, come in. Thank you ever so much for the groceries. Let's put those bags in the kitchen. How much do I owe you?" He reached for his wallet.

"Please Uncle John, it's nothing, really, don't."

"That's awfully kind of you, thank you."

We gave each other a long hug. A whiff of Ben-Gay ointment assaulted my nose as soft notes from a cello welcomed me. He stepped back, held me by my shoulders, and smiled an enthusiastic and warm smile. He was dressed neatly in a white shirt, a buttoned up suit vest, and dark trousers, but he looked awful. There was a scrape on his chin from his fall on the pavement and a bruise on his hand whose color matched his wormlike purple veins. He wore a heavy support brace on his right leg, which, along with an aluminum cane, allowed him to maneuver around the neat, antiquated apartment.

To the right of the entrance was a claustrophobic galley kitchen painted white and lit with garish fluorescent light. A square Timex electric clock, its face dulled with age, hummed at me from the wall. Above it hung an ornate wooden crucifix, complete with the corpus. Beyond the kitchen was a large square living room with a dark brown parquet floor. Against the near wall rested a wood-trimmed Chippendale sofa, its light green cushions covered with yellowed plastic covers that at one time must have been clear. Surrounding the sofa were a coffee table and two end tables whose legs were fluted and capped like Ionic columns. Overlooking the scene from the wall was a triptych oil painting, each panel showing one third of an ancient Roman garden with angels descending from billowing clouds. Two large windows on the adjacent wall were framed with potted plants gorging on warm Manhattan sunlight. Plastic birdfeeders, attached to the sills, awaited diners. Between the windows, sat a well-used phonograph. The album cover nearby said Luigi Boccherini, the source of the lush strings that had welcomed me.

But it was the far wall that commanded my attention. Lining its entire length were dark mahogany bookshelves, filled with every sort of book imaginable: atlases, histories, novels, art compendiums, biographies, and poetry. The fiction and poetry section was in alphabetical order: Borges, Calvino, Proust, Shakespeare, Yeats. Many of the spines were scuffed and covers bent, evidence of fervent and frequent visitation.

The apartment was spotless, surprising for an 83-year-old widower with an injured knee. What was unsurprising to my childhood memories of my uncle was the sense of grace his home possessed. It was a haven of civility and culture, of a man who delighted in the beauty and wonder and wisdom he had found in music, art, and especially literature. And, his most gratifying pleasure, as I would soon learn, was sharing those gifts with anyone who came to visit.

"It's so gracious of you to help an old man. I don't think I'm up to grocery shopping quite yet. I hope I'm not taking you away from anything important."

I feigned indifference. "Don't be silly—it's a subway ride. I'm happy to help. That scrape looks painful."

He laughed off my comment, "Oh, it's fine. I should pay more attention to where I'm walking. It's wonderful to see you. It's been far too long. Sit, sit. So, how've you been? Tell me what's going on in your life."

"I'm doing well. It's good to be back in New York. I'm all settled into my new place downtown on Broome Street, close to my office."

"We can talk about work later. First, the important things. Tell me, is there a young lady in your life?"

"Ah, not at the moment. I was dating a girl in LA, Arden, but . . . well, you know how it goes. Things didn't work out."

"You sound as though you were hoping things *would* work out."

"Well, maybe so. I'm not sure." I took a second to think, not wanting to get into the complexities of our relationship. "I was tired of LA and wanted to come back to New York. There was an opening in my company's office here, but she didn't want to move. So that was that."

Uncle John gazed at me through large wire-framed eyeglasses that on most people would simply sharpen hazy vision, but on my uncle, a man steeped in centuries of books and poetry that told stories of men who contended with their own intolerance and lies and fears in pursuit of power, wealth, fame, and of course, love, his glasses became a silver-rimmed sextant capable of measuring the angles of my heart.

"Why is it that I think there is more to your story?"

I looked down at my shoes with a smile and breathed a muffled laugh. "Arden was wonderful. It didn't end with a fight. We just weren't cut out for each other. She was a Minnesota girl, you know, Midwestern, quiet, modest. Toward the end she just seemed to be unhappy with . . . me, with the way I am, but she was too considerate to make an issue of it. It was complicated."

"Yes, I see, complicated." He rubbed his chin in thought and pointed toward the kitchen. "I was about to have some tea; will you join me?"

"Well, I really should be getting back, I'm having dinner with friends."

"Well, I don't want to spoil your plans. Perhaps just a half cup?" His loose cheeks bounced with his laughter.

I looked at my watch, "Sure, I've got a few minutes."

"Wonderful. How do you like it?"

"Just honey, if you have any, thank you."

I helped him to the kitchen where he poured two small cups of Russian black tea and placed honey, lemon, and several biscotti on a tray, which I carried back to the sofa. He filled a plastic watering can and soaked the philodendrons and dieffenbachias.

"Julian, did Emma ever tell you about her orchids?"

"No, I don't think so."

"Oh, she loved them dearly. She had a tabletop greenhouse. I forget which type she grew, 'epi' something or other. Emma knew them all; I just liked looking at them. What perplexing flowers they were, the humidity, the loose soil and so forth. But, once their eccentricities were understood, the blooms, Julian, oh, they were as magnificent as anything God ever created. When I'd watch Emma tending them, I was reminded of the brilliantly simple thought of the Greek philosopher Plutarch. He said that according to the proverb, good things are hard. He got right to the heart of things, don't you think? And I think he was quite right." And with a laugh he added, "Although, I doubt he was referring to orchids."

I arrived at Uncle John's apartment the following Wednesday evening with his medication and a few groceries. We followed the same routine of tea, biscuits, and conversation. Uncle John was quite a raconteur, as engaging and diverse as the city we lived in. He asked about our favorite music: mine, Coldplay, his, Pavarotti, and surprisingly, John Mayer too! On the question of our favorite novels, I struggled and finally offered up *Catcher in the Rye*, the only book that had any impact on me in high school. His favorite was a worn and well-notated copy of *Don Quixote de la Mancha*, which he delighted in quoting. Then, my 83-year-old uncle jumped forward five hundred years like an 18-year-old to his favorite website, *Arts & Letters Daily*, where he read articles about a variety of subjects from Andrew Wyeth and artificial intelligence to third-world literacy.

Through an open window, the coarse sounds of the traffic on Columbus Avenue sparred with the soft piano of Debussy's *Petite Suite* playing on the phonograph, and our chat drifted as naturally and imperceptibly as the movement of the sun to the topic of Arden.

"Tell me Julian, have you spoken with Arden since leaving Los Angeles?"

"I've thought of calling her, but I'm not sure she wants to talk to me. I don't know how she would react. Honestly, I was ambivalent about leaving LA. I've asked my LA friends how she's doing and if she ever mentions me, but they don't see her as often since I left LA."

"Perhaps you can send her a card. A holiday card, perhaps, or a birthday card. When is her birthday?"

"Actually, it's in a few weeks."

"Splendid! A simple wish for a happy birthday. I'm sure she will appreciate the gesture, and it will let her know you are thinking of her."

"I'm not sure it's a good idea."

"I see. Too personal after your breakup?"

"I don't know. After all that's happened. My head is a mess. I really don't know."

"Julian, if I'm not being intrusive, may I ask the circumstances of your breakup?"

"Ha, are you sure Uncle John? I'm a bit of a neurotic."

"Nonsense. I would like to understand."

"Well, things had built up over the months. Our differences were too ... uh, let's just say that after a while, I felt that she wasn't happy being with me. She began to look embarrassed, upset even, when I'd get irritated about something or other. But she wasn't the type of person to create arguments. She started staying home instead of going out with me, or she'd work more late hours than normal. She was so sweet; she never blamed me, but it was all my fault. I was making her unhappy. Then the job opened in the New York office, and I told her I was going to transfer."

"I see; you felt you were hurting her, so you decided to leave."

"Yes, but she didn't make much of an effort to change my mind. So, I sort of felt it was what she wanted too."

"Well, you did say she was hesitant to start a quarrel."

"Maybe. I don't know. Our personalities were just too different."

As the noise from the street grew louder, Uncle John lowered the window.

"These trucks and ambulances—it seems there are more now than ever. Debussy's piano should be played softly, but I struggle to hear it with all the noise from the street. It's the price of progress I suppose. But, even someone like me, with a disposition more suited to a quieter, simpler time, learns to abide and even appreciate the benefits and the complications of modern life."

He waved away my attempt to help him as he stood and shuffled slowly to the broad facade of books. Without hesitation he pulled a thick volume and began to page through it.

"Julian, in college, along with Mr. Salinger, did you by chance read Alexander Pope?"

"I don't think so. Didn't he write *The Rape of the Lock?*"

"Excellent—I'm impressed. Pope was small of stature, but the substance of his poetry was monumental." My uncle settled on a dogeared page. "When I play a quiet sonata on the stereo, and I hear the turbulence of the street, I think of these lines from his poem 'Windsor Forest':

"But as the world, harmoniously confus'd:

"Where Order in Variety we see,

"And where, tho' all things differ, all agree."

I took a second to think about that. "Harmoniously confused."

He smiled and then his appearance became more earnest. He held his soft, bruised hands a foot apart, palms facing one another as though holding the earth between them and said something that I haven't been able to put out of my mind.

"Yes, the conceit was so proper in Pope's time, that the

miracle of life, from the time of Eden, is in the coexistence of all the variety on earth. So much differs yet there is agreement, a blessed order in the disorder."

The following Sunday, I blew off an afternoon with friends at a local brewery and rode up to see my uncle. He had said his knee was feeling better, so we planned a short walk to Central Park. When I arrived at his apartment, he was filling a backpack.

I reminded him, "We're just going to the park, Uncle John."

"It's an old habit. Emma and I walked in Central Park often, and backpacks were convenient. Plus, it made us feel like school children again. We would pack a piece of fruit or some nuts to snack on, and Emma would carry her binoculars to spy woodpeckers and cardinals. Your Aunt Emma was quite the romantic. We weren't much older than you when she asked a young couple walking in the park to take our picture under the statue of Romeo and Juliet. We imitated the lovers' pose, our arms like the long necks of a pair of doting swans, encircling one another. And we always brought something to read. Emma liked the *New York Times*, and I would bring a notebook and whatever book I happened to be reading at the time. You know, Robert Louis Stevenson said he always carried two books in his pocket, one to read and one to write in."

"You must miss her very much. Has it been difficult for you, these past years?"

"You never get over the longing completely. But I take

comfort. I know I will see her again." He paused, motionless, looking into his backpack and said, "Right alongside Philip."

Outside on 84th Street, it was as though Aunt Emma's spirit had been listening to her husband. She brought to my memory her own story of the romantic she had married, a story she had shared with me at their fiftieth wedding anniversary party just before I left for LA. She showed me a letter Uncle John had written to her celebrating the event. In it, he quoted Elizabeth Browning, "I love thee with the breath, smiles, tears, of all my life." He ended the letter saying that Emma was "as vital to him as the air he breathed." No man in my life, not my father, certainly not Uncle Vic or Uncle Sonny, had ever said such a profound thing.

As we arrived at the park, our conversation turned to a subject that was not unexpected, and admittedly, I welcomed it: Arden.

"Julian, have you given further thought to the idea of a birthday card?"

"I've thought about it, but I'm still not sure."

"Forgive me, I tend to become a nosy uncle on such matters. I should leave this to your own good judgment."

"No, Uncle John, really, I don't mind talking about it. I just don't know if she wants to hear from me."

"In my long and blessed life, I have found it helpful to talk about one's feelings, and I'm a very good listener."

"I enjoy our talks, Uncle John. I think Arden would enjoy your company, too: your calm, your interests, your thoughtfulness. I've always thought you were a unique person in our family. In some ways, Arden is unique too. You know, she's been very successful in her work, high-pressure work. But what really inspired me was her ability to be both assertive and considerate at once. You don't meet many goodhearted people doing billion dollar merger deals. They're mostly like me, impatient and inflexible. You know, forget the other guy's feelings, just do the deal, and pocket the profit."

"Oh, come now, you diminish yourself. I'm sure you weren't so overbearing. After all, a nice girl like Arden saw something worthwhile in you."

"Yes, I loved to do things for her. And I could make her laugh in any moment. For a while anyway."

"You mentioned once that she had Scandinavian roots. Was it Norway?"

"Yes, her grandparents were from Sandvika, Norway, near Oslo. We had talked about traveling there."

"I've never been to Norway, but many years ago, Emma and I visited Stockholm and Reykjavik. They are marvelous cities with delightful, robust people. In fact, I'm reading a wonderful novel titled *Independent People*, written by an Icelander, a Nobel laureate, by the name of Halldor Laxness. I have it here in my bag. It's a lovely and brutal story that follows the life and hard times of an Icelandic sheep farmer named Bjartur. He's the most confounding character, cynical and demanding yet noble and appealing. He insists, to the detriment of his family, on remaining independent of all others while living in a harsh land that requires interdependence. His intransigence wreaks havoc on his friends and family. I'm rooting for Bjartur to find a path toward balance."

He pulled the book out of his backpack and showed me the cover.

"I'm nearly finished, and you're welcome to borrow it if you think it might interest you."

"Well, I'm not much of a reader, but it sounds like an interesting premise. Maybe I'll give it a try."

"Good, you should try to read more. Thoreau said that books are the treasured wealth of the world. Sometimes, in my melancholy, I think I'm the only one in the world who feels the way I do. Then, I find a character in a book who shows me I'm not alone at all."

Back at his apartment, as Uncle John freshened up, I put the tea kettle on the stove and made my way into the living room, a room completely foreign to the contemporary vibe of my new apartment, yet somehow, I had become very comfortable here among my uncle's books. I wondered how a person came to be like my uncle. Was it some fixed genetic code only available to a lucky few? Or was it the result of parents and teachers, friends and an environment that prized culture and learning? I thought of his interest in literature as I scanned the landscape of books. I imagined it as a vast source of nourishment for my uncle like a boundless and fertile pasture rich with human understanding; a pasture of knowledge that, regardless of genetics, everyone had access to during their lives, in school or in libraries; a pasture to which I had never paid any attention until my reunion with Uncle John.

He emerged from his room wearing a light blue shirt and navy sweater vest.

"Uncle John, I have a thought."

"Yes. What is it"

"I was thinking that maybe I could come by to visit you on a more regular basis. You know, just to talk, have lunch, visit a museum, maybe take walks in the park. I was thinking of buying a new backpack."

Once again, his soft cheeks danced with delight, "What a marvelous idea, if you're sure I won't bore you to death."

A week later, Uncle John, walking robustly on his own, folded himself into the passenger seat of my rental car for the drive to Staten Island to celebrate Uncle Vic and Aunt Teddi's fifty-fifth anniversary. We stopped at an art shop downtown where I was having an old family photo of the two framed as a gift. I was greeted with an apology from the shopkeeper.

"Hi, Mr. Serra. I'm so sorry, but your photo isn't ready. My assistant Tom has been out sick the past two days and then my large joiner broke. I was going to call to let you know it wouldn't be ready."

I looked at his frazzled, sweaty brow and said, "Yeah, that's a problem. I need it today."

"I know, I'm so sorry, I'm going to take 15 percent off the price."

"I appreciate that, but it really doesn't solve my problem."

"I feel terrible. I'll get it done as soon as I can. I'm going to work through the night."

"Tell you what, why don't you just call me when it's ready and I'll ship it to my aunt and uncle. It'll be a belated anniversary gift."

"Oh, Mr. Serra, thank you so much."

"And don't take anything off the price."

"Are you sure? It's the least I can do."

"No, no, full price."

"Well then, how about I deliver it to you when it's ready?"

"That would be great. I'm just over on Broome; you have my address."

"Thanks again for understanding. I wish more customers were like you."

"No problem. Have a good day. Oh, and I hope your assistant Tom is feeling better."

Uncle John was waiting in the car, and I signaled that I'd be another minute as I headed to the stationery store down the street. When I returned to the car, Uncle John and I signed an oversized pop-up anniversary card, and I tossed it on the back seat along with a bottle of sparkling wine from Napa and a birthday card with no message inside, just a big blank space to write in.

ACKNOWLEDGMENTS

One of my intentions in writing these stories was to share a part of myself with the people I love, especially my children and grandchildren. To my family, I offer my heartfelt thanks for their steady and loving encouragement during the writing of this book.

It is impossible to overstate my appreciation of Matthew Sharpe, whose editing skill and perceptive literary vision were an invaluable source of positive energy. My thanks to him for helping to make this book the best it could be.

For their inspiring support, thoughtful feedback, and generous camaraderie, sincere thanks to my fellow writers at the Brandywine Valley Writers Group and Wordwrights Writers Group in Chester County, Pennsylvania.

To my longtime friend Ed McCann, a special thank you for providing guidance and optimism when I needed it most.

Many thanks to Colin Rolfe at Epigraph Publishing for his artful work in designing and rendering this book and to Laura Matthews for her meticulous care in copyediting.

As any writer knows, writing and rejection are zealous and inseparable partners. To the editors at *The Muleskinner Journal*, *Umbrella Factory Magazine*, and *Bloom*, my abiding gratitude for publishing my fiction

I enjoy hearing from readers.
Please send me a note at callarofiction@gmail.com

www.ingramcontent.com/pod-product-compliance
Lightning Source LLC
Chambersburg PA
CBHW030125260626
47156CB00008B/2794